Inside the Pages and Other Stories

Nightmares can be real

Van Lawrence Umerez

Ukiyoto Publishing

All global publishing rights are held by

Ukiyoto Publishing

Published in 2022

Content Copyright © Van Lawrence Umerez

ISBN 9789364946285

All rights reserved.

No part of this publication may be reproduced, transmitted, or stored in a retrieval system, in any form by any means, electronic, mechanical, photocopying, recording or otherwise, without the prior permission of the publisher.

The moral rights of the author have been asserted.

This is a work of fiction. Names, characters, businesses, places, events, locales, and incidents are either the products of the author's imagination or used in a fictitious manner. Any resemblance to actual persons, living or dead, or actual events is purely coincidental.

This book is sold subject to the condition that it shall not by way of trade or otherwise, be lent, resold, hired out or otherwise circulated, without the publisher's prior consent, in any form of binding or cover other than that in which it is published.

To Krishmar Llorin

Contents

Inside the Pages	1
Chapter 1	2
Chapter 2	3
Chapter 3	7
Chapter 4	8
Chapter 5	11
Chapter 6	12
Chapter 7	16
Chapter 8	29
Chapter 9	41
Chapter 10	43
Chapter 11	44
Chapter 12	53
Confession	54
Chapter 1	55
Chapter 2	60
Chapter 3	66
Chapter 4	67
Chapter 5	69
Chapter 6	75
Chapter 7	76
Chapter 8	77

Enclosed	78
Chapter 1	79
Chapter 2	83
Chapter 3	87
Chapter 4	94
Chapter 5	96
Chapter 6	100
Freebie	102
Chapter 1	103
Chapter 2	109
Chapter 3	111
Chapter 4	113
Chapter 5	118
Chapter 6	122
Chapter 7	125
Chapter 8	128
Chapter 9	132
Chapter 10	136
Chapter 11	139
Chapter 12	141
Chapter 13	149
Diary	151
Chapter 1	152

Chapter 2	156
Chapter 3	164
Chapter 4	180
Chapter 5	181
Chapter 6	183
About the Author	184

Inside the Pages

Chapter 1

The sunlight kisses my face as my fingers continuously hit the keys of the keyboard of my laptop. My gaze shifts from the keyboard to the screen from time to time. My lips move imperceptibly. My wrists press against the edge of my laptop.

I'm writing the 29th chapter of my novel. I still can't think of a title for the story, but I usually worry about that matter more after I finish the first draft. The title of my previous books only contains one word, of course, excluding the word "The." I'm planning the same format with this one I'm currently working on.

Chapter 2

I began writing when I was nineteen years old. I was a college student taking BSIT course. I lived in an apartment near the university with my friend Pablo. He was an Engineering student and dreamt of working with a prominent company, which he didn't reach because three years after Graduation, Cancer took his life painfully.

Despite my lack of a generous amount of extra money, I still had the guts to buy a lot of books; I just got to look for cheaper copies at a book sale or second hand book stores. At that time, I'd always set aside a specific amount of money I'd spend on books for a month, which was nearly a quarter of my weekly allowance. I could buy three books with that. Four if I got lucky.

On a Sunday morning, I went early to a second hand bookstore and found a beat-up but cheap copy of Cormac McCarthy's novel The Road. I finished it the same day and it was amazing. That book made me fell in love with reading, or literature in general.

The day after reading that amazing book, I began to write a story as a practice. It's about an unnamed man who woke up on a post-apocalyptic earth. You'll see the heavy influence of McCarthy's novel. I only wrote two pages of that story; then I began another one, then another. I had my friends read my stories and very few of them actually liked my works. Most of them didn't understand a thing. A professor of mine read a short story I wrote called *Project Metamorphosis*. It's about a group of scientists who kidnaps beggars on the streets and conduct experiments on them, turning them into deadly Cyborgs for the Government. My professor said the premise was interesting (not necessarily original), but the prose needed a lot more work.

During my remaining days as a College Student, I'd always find an opportunity to write, usually before bedtime. Pablo, my roommate, would always tell me to sleep.

"For god's sake, it's one in the morning already. Get some shut eyes," he'd say.

"Yeah. Just one more chapter." I'd say, then sip a bitter coffee.

"We have an exam tomorrow. Know your priorities," he'd reply as he covers himself fully with his smelly blanket.

"Yes. I know my priorities," and my calloused fingers would continue to hit the keys on my keyboard. *Tak-a-taktak-a-taktak-tak-tak*.

I finished my BSIT course without any honor, but I couldn't care less.

I finally went home. After a week of rest, I began locking myself in my room and writing my first full length novel. My room was quiet except for the sound of the keyboard and the sound the electric fan makes. I don't listen to music while I work. I don't understand those writers who prefer it. But to each his own.

One afternoon, while writing a steamy bed scene for my first horror novel, my mother went to my room (real good timing) and told me to start finding a *real* job. "You're old. Soon you'll have to get your own life, and you'll need to work."

"But ma, I'm already working." I said, pointing at the screen, hoping for the pages of the document to be zoomed out enough for it to be illegible.

"But it's not a real job. Find one that's related to the course you've finished. Apply for work to big companies, schools, or something."

I promised her I'd get the story I was writing published. The royalty may not be as big as the salary in an IT job, but probably enough to pay for bills and books. As a BSIT student who hated my course to the core, I'd be a fool to get an IT job. It's like entering a prison for the second time, or hell, in that matter.

Years went on and I still hadn't published anything. I would wait weeks and months just to receive a rejection letter. Some wouldn't even send one. So to help with the expenses in the house, with the money I borrowed from a friend, I established my first business. After a year of operation, I was able to return the borrowed money and help with the house bills and other financial responsibilities. I was earning a decent income.

Between those hours of running my business, I would open my laptop and start typing. I did a pretty good job of being patient with the customers who interrupted me while I was writing an important plot point.

> *...he brought down the knife repeatedly with an unidentifiable pattern. Hot blood splashed on his face. Drool fell from his mouth. He utte*

"How much for the Spanish bread?" a customer would say.

After three years of managing a Bakery, a publisher finally accepted a manuscript I submitted. It's a sixty-thousand-word novel called The Church Usher. It's about, well, a church usher, who, at night, fights fallen angels while he himself is a fallen angel. It deals with redemption or something. That kick-started my career as a professional writer. I wrote books that sold a decent number of copies, and I wrote books that became laughing-stocks, but the former was dominant. I attended book signings. I signed thousands of books. That smell of ink as I write my autograph on the first page of my book, and the sound that friction between the tip of the pen and the surface of the paper produces stays with me.

I met a girl at a book convention. We became friends, then later led to a romantic relationship. She got tired of me and then our shared love ended badly. Then I wrote more wonders and mysteries.

Chapter 3

I began writing this novel on my 32nd birthday. It would be a *slasher* novel, and the perspective will shift from the past to the present in a continuous manner. The story tells the struggles of a group of teens that began when they accidentally ran over and killed a school bully in a deserted road at night. The father of the bully, a corrupt City Mayor, hires a hitman who happened to be a psychopath. I still don't know what will happen because I didn't write a plot. I'm what they call a "Pantser."

Of all my books, this would probably be my favorite. It's not special or anything. The concept is not new. I can't explain why I believe this would be my best work.

Chapter 4

I created the antagonist in my mind while attending the funeral of my uncle. The funeral was conducted in a church. After the priest finished his tedious sermon, he asked among the audience if someone would like to give a message or some sort of eulogy the star of the show wouldn't hear. My uncle's youngest son went on stage. He talked about how much he loved his father, his father that he refused to take care of in his dying days because he was with his friend and was having a blast; he talked about how he misses him yada yada blah blah blah cry, made those fake tears flow from his ugly eyes yada yadayada and all that crap.

After the eulogies, the priest asked the attendees to take a look at my uncle to pay our respects. I went first because I planned to leave early for another book signing event at a mall nearby. My primary purpose for going to that city was because of that book signing event. Uncle's funeral just happened to be in the same City, so I stopped by to meet with my relatives and, you know, to be polite.

Behind me was a weeping old lady; she had curly, short hair. I still can't forget that disgusting sound every time she sniffed her dripping snot.

So I took a look at my uncle behind the glass of the coffin. You ask me what was in my mind? Definitely not the memories I had with the bastard, that time when he forced me to try a cigarette, or that time when he pulled down my shorts while I was singing James Ingram's *Just Once* in Karaoke. So no, I didn't remember any pleasant memories with this dead meat in the coffin. Don't get me wrong, I don't loathe him.

What's in my mind was another idea for a novel. I saw my uncle's dead, white face, his lack of expression, and his way of lying inside the coffin – erect. So what if I create an antagonist that has a white complexion, almost like a corpse's? An antagonist that always stands oddly erect. An antagonist that bears no expression on his face: a face like a mannequin's. Yeah. I found it a pretty good idea.

Even during that book signing event, I couldn't stop thinking about the concept. *And he's gonna be a psychopath, a man that feels no remorse, no emotion, no empathy, exactly like a dead person. Yep. Not original, but a good concept, nonetheless.*

When I went home, I took a nap, and when I woke up, I immediately went to my working space and opened my laptop. I began writing my ideas. I don't always take notes because I believe that's where I get bad ideas. But this time, I just couldn't help it. I wrote down the ideas not to prevent myself from forgetting it, but to simply have the pleasure of writing it down.

I glued my eyes to what I wrote, then I smiled.

Chapter 5

The next day or two, I began writing the novel in which this new antagonist of mine would lurk. Every time I lay in bed, I just couldn't take the picture out of my mind; his expressionless face looking through a window, or looking straight into your soul as he walks slowly towards you. These kinds of scenarios always bring shivers down my spine, but excitement mostly.

I tapped the keys of my keyboard with utter excitement. Every page where my antagonist makes an appearance, my fingers just seemed to move faster, faster than my mind.

Chapter 6

I finish the 29th chapter and get to do what my mother would say a *real* work. The royalties from the sales of my books apparently are not enough to keep my bills paid, so I actually followed my mother's advice to get an IT job. I work as an IT teacher at Senior High School. I teach programming using the language Java for the first and second semesters. Despite being busy with this job, I still manage to save some time for writing. If sacrificing my time of sleep will be required, I won't hesitate to do it.

I open my laptop and check the assigned outputs of my students. To my relief, most of them appear to be doing well. Some are getting behind, so there'll be the need to help them catch up. After checking and noting feedbacks to each work, I resume writing. I look at the time on my phone and it's quarter to 10 already.

I open the file and begin typing for my novel again, starting with the 30th chapter. There's the scene when one of the major characters, Richard, encounters the unnamed villain while taking a walk with his dog. That time Richard is already a grown-up. He is confident that they defeated the persistent killer during their younger years, so he feels safe now. But oh boy, how wrong he is. He's in an oval, alone. It is already morning but the sky is not yet bright. The sun is still hiding in the horizon.

> *He jogged while loosely holding the leash of his dog, a German Shepherd named Sarah. She was keeping up with his pace.*
>
> *There's no sound in the oval but his heavy breathing and the singing choir of the crickets. He's thinking about expanding the business he's operating to a couple of towns when in the corner of his vision he saw a silhouette of a man. He turned his head in that direction and realized it's just a tree. Its shape was like a man crucified on an invisible cross. It's not the shape he saw in the corner of his field of vision.*
>
> *"Must be the pills," he said quietly, and looked down at Sarah. The dog regarded him with her beautiful eyes.*

I stop and grab my cup of coffee with shaking hands. I sip and feel a slight comfort when the hot coffee flows in my throat. I cross my arms and rest my back and stare at the white screen and the blinking line at the end of the last sentence I wrote. I rub my eyes with my cold palms and yawn. I stare at my work for another two minutes, then start to type again.

> *He massaged his temples with his thumb and index finger, then continued to jog. Inside his head,* Sweet Dreams *by* Eurythmics *was*

playing. He forgot to bring his headphones so he's got to play music on his own. After the second stanza, the song immediately shifted to Billy Joel's Piano Man.

I stop writing, stand up, and go to the bathroom and empty my bladder. I flush the toilet and go back to my desk. I stare at the blinking line for a few seconds before I resume typing.

As the lyrics of the song reached the beginning of the last round of chorus, he heard footsteps. No, not just steps. Someone was jogging approximately five meters behind him. Sarah turned to the other jogger's direction, stopped for a second with ears pricked, and then went on jogging again as she saw she's being left by her owner. Richard turned to look behind him and saw the jogger. He raised a hand as a greeting and went on jogging. He couldn't explain why, but his pace increased.

Yeah. It's not the pills, *he thought.* He must be the silhouette I saw before. *This gave him relief. The pills he's taking were not showing any side effect.*

The Beatles' Penny Lane *was now playing in his head.*

I stop again. I am struggling to continue. I yawn, stretch my arms, and wipe my eyes. I just want to stop writing. I want to save my progress and turn off the laptop. But there is the urge to continue typing, and the urge to stop writing. This mixed feeling gives me discomfort and confusion.

I have the urge to continue because I feel like it's my responsibility, like working on my capstone, or teaching my students, or taking care of my sick wife (if I have one). It feels like something will go wrong if I stop.

The urge to stop writing is not caused by exhaustion, but fear. That feeling like, if I continue, something unpleasant will happen, like fiddling with a working code, or fixing an appliance I have no knowledge of. This urge is from me, that, I am sure. The former, I don't think so.

The latter gets the best of me and I save my work and close my laptop with tremendous effort fighting that unusual resistance, like not eating delicious pasta that is served on the table while on a low-carb diet. It is hard to stop, but I succeed anyway.

Chapter 7

Morning comes. I choose to give myself a break from writing the novel. Suddenly, I want to completely stop writing. I go to the mall and intend to enjoy my time there. And when I say enjoying my time in a mall, I mean in a bookstore. I look at the shelves, read a few pages, look at the *about the author* sections, and purchase anything that interests me. I come out of the bookstore with ten new books.

After that, I buy a ticket and watch an adaptation of a book written by one of my favorite authors. I've been meaning to watch that movie on a streaming platform, but I think I can try watching it in the cinema. It's been a long time since I watched a movie on a big screen together with many viewers.

After watching, I eat in food courts, go to toy stores, comic book stores, and other stores that's not as boring as a clothing store. I return to the bookstore and buy another two books.

When I feel the exhaustion of walking with heavy books in both hand, the mild pain in the small of my back, and the weakening of my legs, I decide to go home and take a rest. I promise myself to take the whole day as a break. I will not open my laptop to continue writing. I'm not going to take a look at our next lesson. Heck, I'm not even going to sit at my working desk.

Around 7:00pm, I wake up and fix myself a dinner – country-style omelet, my favorite. After I finish my meal, I open the television and play a newly-released movie that's three-hours long. I can't stand it, so I turn off the TV after half an hour. It's not that the movie is bad. I just don't feel like watching right now.

I go to the bathroom and wash my face. I look at myself in the reflection of the mirror; the beads of water run down my face; they drop from my chin and from the tip of my nose. I don't know what's happening to me. I feel something in my head, like that tiring feeling in my arms after hours of holding my bag of books. I lower my head again in the sink and splash myself with cold water, this time wiping my face briskly with the rough palm of my hands. During those few moments that my eyes are closed, something flashes inside my mind, like a Powerpoint slide that abruptly appears then proceeds to the end of the slide that is full black. I'm pretty sure my mind didn't generate that image, which was unusually vivid. I was thinking of something else as I washed my face, my new books specifically. That horrifying image came from something else. It makes my heart beat faster, almost painfully, and the hairs of my arms and nape stand up. The image is that of a man; the face is white; any expression is absent, like a mannequin, like a dead person whose eyes are opened.

Well, I think, *it's the antagonist I created.* As a writer, I think it's normal for images that concern my work-in-progress books to involuntarily appear in my mind from time to time. It's normal. Yes. This chilling feeling is normal. Of course, my creation is scary and realistic; it's supposed to scare even me. I let out a chuckle, then wash my face for the third time while struggling to keep my eyes open. No image appears this time.

I feed my eyes with the books I bought, looking at the covers, sometimes for a full minute. I put them on my bookshelf along with my unread books. From that shelf I take a mass market paperback copy of Robert Ludlum's *Bourne Identity*. I read a couple of pages, then stop. I can't stand reading either, so I close the book and put it on my nightstand carelessly.

I lay in my bed and pull my blanket up to my chest. I close my eyes and urge myself to sleep because I have work tomorrow. Being late will not help with my performance as a teacher. I need to sleep.

To dream of the old happy days...

This gave him relief...

happy memories of my childhood.

The pills he's taking were not showing any side effect...

life before this solitude...

The Beatles' Penny Lane was now playing in his head...

...or fantasies will do...

Penny Lane was now...

...or nightmares... nightmares are okay...

...was now playing in his head...

...was now playing...

...now playing...

...in his head...

"DAMN IT!"

I throw the covers and get up while continuously swearing under my breath. That feeling hits me again, the contradicting urge, to stop or to go on, and the latter wins this time. I go to my desk and stare at my laptop, felling another round of chills. With a trembling hand, I reach to touch it. It feels oddly cold at the tips of my fingers.

I breathe deeply, letting out a loud sigh.

As I open my laptop, my heart beats faster again; pounding against my chest. There's this unexplainable feeling, feeling of terror. Opening my laptop feels like opening a coffin with a rotting corpse inside, ready to grab me by the neck with its rotting hand and disgusting fingers and drag me to where it's been lying. There is no rotting corpse when I open my laptop; there's only the light that flashes in my face, the flash of light I should be used to seeing after years of working using this device. But this night that flash of light feels unfamiliar, alien.

I open a folder.

Inside, alone, at the upper right corner of the window, is the file named NEW NOVEL UNTITLED FIRST DRAFT 2020. I touch the touchpad with the tip of my right middle finger and it sends a jolting shock through my body, except it doesn't. It's just my imagination. I drag the cursor to the file and tap the touchpad twice. The file opens. A pop-up appears, a few seconds of loading passes, and the first page displays itself. In the upper part, UNTITLED is written. Center Alignment. A few enters below that, is my pen name.

I scroll down the document; paragraphs of words become almost a blur until I reach my latest progress.

The Beatles' Penny Lane *was now playing in his head.*

At the end of the sentence is the text cursor, blinking as though in greeting. I stare at it, counting exactly twenty blinks before I start typing.

> *At the beginning of the first chorus, Richard turned his head in the other jogger's direction. He's gone. Richard stopped jogging and surveyed the whole place. The sun still refused to give light to the sky so he could barely see a thing. He's not able to see any sign of the other jogger. Confusion started to circulate in his mind. He continued to jog, and this time, he forbade his mind from generating any music.*

Another stop. I go to the kitchen, take a pitcher of water, and pour some in a glass. I drink and my dry mouth and throat become moist. I return to my working place and place my hands on the keyboard.

> *After approximately five minutes, he stopped by a rusty bleacher and sat there. Sarah sat beside him. He stroked the back of her head.*
> *"You wanna go home?"*
> *The dog looked at him in reply.*
> *"Let's just rest for a few minutes, okay?"*

My fingers gain speed.

> *Right after he finished that sentence, he heard a rustle in the grass where the bleacher was mounted. He turned to the source of the sound, and saw no one's there. He looked up at the sky and knew that the day's prologue would begin shortly.*
>
> *He leaned back, his shoulder resting on the seat above the one he's sitting on, and closed his eyes and breathed calmly. He hummed a song he couldn't recognize.*
>
> *He opened his eyes and sat bolt upright when he heard Sarah's painful whine, followed by a soft thump in the grass. The German Shepherd was now lying on the ground. The blades of grass near the dog's brown fur are now dark red instead of green. He stood up, almost tumbling, and crouched near the dog. He looked around and saw a man standing straight like a post; a*

couple of meters away from him. He couldn't see the man's face, but he could see the somehow glinting blade of a knife the man was holding, dark liquid dropped from its edge to the ground.

He stood up awkwardly. His heart began to pound against his chest and his limbs began to tremble. "What did you do?" he said. He's not sure if he was able to actually sound the question out. His throat seemed to dry in an instant.

The ominous figure didn't answer. By his discretion, the man's a body builder or a heavy worker. He could see the bulging muscles underneath the man's clothing.

He looked at his whining dog. His mouth curved downward; his eyes became wet. A mixture of sorrow and terror hugged him tightly. "What the hell did you do?" he asked again. This time, he's sure the man heard him.

He averted his gaze from the man to his only companion in life right now. Sarah's chest rose one more time before her breathing stopped. Her eyes and mouth were open.

He shouldn't have stood up. He should've stayed and caressed her head until her life faded. Hell, he didn't even try to save her. He only stood frozen. His fear of the man with the bloodied knife conquered him.

"Oh god, no..." hot tears flowed from his eyes. "What have you done? Who are you?"

The man remained silent and tranquil, like a statue.

"Answer me!"

When he received silence in reply again, his fear was replaced with a rage he had never felt before. He desired to rip this man's head off more than anything else. He broke his paralysis and ran toward the murderer, shouting profanities with every step in the green grass.

Then rage was replaced with total shock when the man with the knife ran toward him. Richard was expecting him to be still and wait until he reaches him, but the man ran head on with unexpected speed.

The blade of the knife plunged squarely into Richard's neck, his blood mixing with his dog's. The man pulled the knife from his neck swiftly, and blood flowed from his vital wound and mouth to his body. He felt the heat and the wetness of it. When authorities discovered his body, his white t-shirt would be almost entirely maroon. He clutched his neck, trying to close the wound, strangling himself in the process. He tried to talk but failed. Instead, he made a gurgling sound as he fell to the ground, eyes wide open. His head fell on a small rock hidden among the blades of grass.

I stop. I breathe deeply, as if I jogged myself. I look at the clock. It was 10:02pm. Despite the terror I've been unusually feeling lately this day, I feel relief when I write down something. Maybe I can finally sleep peacefully.

I was thinking of using a gun instead of a knife with my villain's first kill after more than a decade. But I thought against it. A gun would be too convenient. A knife would do the job of bringing more horror and gore. That's why Alfred Hitchcock's *Psycho* works with the audience, and so are the *Halloween* and *Scream* Franchise.

The place of the murder is a real place. It's an oval inside the campus where I finished my course. I used to jog there with my classmates. The rusty bleacher's real too. Whenever I sat there, my shorts (or jogging pants sometimes) always had a stain that would be fricking hard to wash off. While typing, every detail I remember in the place was clear as if I'm actually there.

I try to stand up but fail, my fingers still on the keyboard. My wrists begin to hurt as they are pressing on the edge of the Laptop; that kind of position always leaves a brown spot on the outer side of each of my wrists. Again, I order my hands to leave the keyboard, but they refuse to follow. I can move my fingers freely within the keyboard's premise; I just can't get my hands off it completely.

The couple of contradicting urge stir in me again, but this time, the urge to continue is a lot stronger than the urge to stop, to lay down, to take a rest, and to sleep. Something tells me I should finish something; maybe a couple of paragraphs or more. I want to stop, but I can't.

My fingers begin to work.

> *The sky starts to brighten, but the sun is still hiding. Maybe it had already woken up and just been stretching before showing itself.*
>
> *The man looked at what he's done. He looked at it like an artwork he had worked on for years. He felt like Leonardo Da Vinci looking at his painting* Mona Lisa. *Satisfaction bloomed inside him. He couldn't help smiling.*

Oh god, I want to stop, but I can't. My fingers and the backs of my hands start to hurt more, feels like a drill is making holes on my flesh.

> *He inspected the surroundings with his watchful eyes. The trees, the bleachers, the fences made of wires.*

The tapping sound of the keyboard becomes louder and louder, like a hammer hitting a nail.

> *No one saw what he did, because if someone did, he's going to have another job, which he did not desire.*

Oh god. I do not intend to write these sentences.

> *When he was confident that there were no witnesses, he causally walked toward his green van. His steps barely made a noise. His target had not heard him approaching; even the dog, whose sense of hearing was probably a lot better,*

was unaware. Throughout the years, he mastered the art of silence and tranquility; that is his asset. The priest, the carpenter, the street sweeper, the congressman, and many other individuals thought they were alone.

My fingers continue tapping the keys with speed I never imagined to have. Beads of sweat to come out of the pores of my face and my throat becomes dry as desert.

A few meters from his van, he stopped and turned around as if someone had poked him in the shoulder. He's pretty sure no one was in here, but he still had this odd feeling of being watched, and someone actually saw what he did, or was watching him while he's hiding behind the trees.

He looked to his right and finally saw the spectator. He stares at you with those dead eyes.

I never intended to write this novel in second POV.

He is studying you, looking through your skin and into your shivering soul. You thought he wouldn't see you, didn't you? Well, you're wrong. He was feeling your presence during his previous works; he just couldn't put a finger on it until now.

When he killed his mother, you were there. When he strangled the priest with a rosary, you were also there. You heard every crushing sound as he bashed the carpenter's head with a hammer. You heard the shriek of the whore as she burned down and was reduced to charred meat. You heard the prayers of one of the main characters, what's his name? Lewis? Is that right? Yes. You heard his prayers that did nothing. His god didn't save him from the devil incarnate you created.

He leaves no witnesses.

He walks toward you with a straight face. Slowly at first, then gaining speed at the tenth step. He grips the handle of the knife tightly and raises it and

With tremendous effort and a pinch of miracle, I jerk my hands off the keyboard and stand up immediately as soon as I make sure I'm in control again, knocking down my chair backward. My whole body's trembling like a phone receiving messages while in silent mode.

"Oh my god," I utter.

I stare at the blinking cursor for a couple of seconds, almost hypnotizing myself with it, and close my laptop. No, I slam it, not worrying if the next time I open it, there would be cracks on the screen.

I go to the kitchen and drink two full glasses of cold water. I lean forward against the counter with my hands and arms supporting my wait. I remain in that position for quite a while, waiting for the pounding in my chest to subside and my breathing to become normal. Once I felt okay, I return to my room and lay in my bed. My bed feels uncomfortable.

I cover myself with the blanket up to my neck. I feel cold.

I close my eyes and try to empty my mind, but I failed. The words are tattooed on the surface of the walls of my mind. I didn't type those words. Those weren't from me. It seemed like my fingers had a mind of their own.

And I don't write from a second person point of view because it won't fit the story. Why did I write those sentences? I ask myself. Who's the *you?* I don't know any characters that might refer to that. It's not me. It shouldn't be me. Oh hell no. Not me. He's not coming after me, is he? That's impossible. No nono. He only exists inside the pages of my novel. It's impossible for him to step out of a paper that's not even printed yet.

Who's the witness?
Who?
Who's the *you?*

Chapter 8

I have tuna and leftover rice for breakfast. Not the most pleasant meal, but still better than leafy foods.

I am feeling something in my head, like it's being opened as though I'm a corpse undergoing autopsy. The pain subsided a little when I have a sip of my morning coffee. I don't know if it's supposed to work that way, but at least it works.

In every chew of the cold rice and oily fish, the words seem to be being typed inside my head. I can almost hear the faint sound of clacking. *Tak-a-tak-tak.*

The excitement of writing was completely gone that night. What remained are fear and the feeling of obligation. I never felt like that before. Whenever I write a story, it always feels like talking and laughing with a lover (despite the common struggles of writing). Now, it feels like I'm working in a prison under the angry sun.

As I wash the plate and utensils after I eat, the feeling of helplessness retrieves itself from my memory. When my hands worked on their own last night, disturbing possibilities occurred in my mind. While I'm washing this plate, what if my right hand just decides to promptly grab the knife in the nearby knife block, then slit my throat while my blood splashes on the white plate I'm washing? That's how he murdered his mother, the antagonist I created, I mean. But my hands look to be in my control right now. No funny or strange feeling.

All of this must have been a hallucination, I think. I don't know how I obtained this crap. I didn't and don't take any pills or any form of drugs. Alcohol, maybe? No, I didn't drink alcohol for the last two years. I don't know what caused it, but it must have been something I consumed; I just don't know what in the blue hell it is.

I wipe my hand briskly then go to my room. The laptop sits at my desk calmly, as if waiting for something, or somebody. I slowly walk towards it. Yes, sure, there's still the feeling of dread, but it's less bad than last night.

I open it and the light at the screen flashes again, now faint in the daylight coming through my room's window. The last page where I typed my progress appeared, almost like a jump scare in a movie. I bring my face closer to the screen and squint a little.

It's real, alright. Real as the Holocaust, or 9/11.

He grips the handle of the knife tightly and raises it and

And then what? What would he do if my fingers went on typing? He'll swing the knife downward? Then my head will split open? No, not my head. Like I said, it can't be me.

The text cursor greets me again with its blinking line. I drag the mouse cursor to it and highlight the end of the latest paragraph to the beginning of the paragraph about the man walking towards his green van. I try to blur those words in my vision as the blue highlight does its job, but the words are clear, screaming in my face. The two seconds of selecting the sentences feels painfully forever. There's a weak resistance in the back of my hand as I press the backspace key. The sound that it makes brings me relief. Something loosens in my chest. I let out a sigh and end the chapter with what remains. The next chapter will be about the residents and authorities finding Richard's and Sarah's bodies on the ground in the center of the oval. A young jogger would find it, or maybe the school guard. I'll decide later. Richard's wife will cry her eyes out when she learns what happened to her husband. A major character and one of Richard's friends named Pablo (I named him after my former and late roommate and friend) will arrive at the scene. He too, will shed some tears for his friend. This will be an emotional chapter, and this is what I'll work on next, as soon as I have the courage to work again.

I need to talk to somebody, to unwind.

I take my phone and call Sarah, one of my colleagues and my closest friend. We're both teachers. I work in a High School; she works in a University.

"Maybe around 5:00 o'clock?" I say on the phone.

"After my class. It's usually done by 4 in the afternoon."

"My class ends early on Mondays, so I'm free anytime after noon," she replies. "Just call me when you're ready."

"Okay. Thanks."

"Bye."

I wear my uniform, prepare my things, and go on. It takes me ten minutes to arrive at school. From the distance, I see the guard checking a student's backpack. I don't know if it's caused by the lighting from the sun; his face looks pale as if blood ran out from him. But as I walk nearing his post, his white pigmentation fades and his face is in normal complexion again.

"Good morning, sir," the guard says, smiling.

"Good morning," I say. "May I ask, do you have Anemia?"

"Sir?" he replied, puzzled.

"Oh, I'm sorry. Never mind."

"Well, sir, I was diagnosed with something else. But it's not Anemia."

"Oh, yes. Sorry. It just blurted... you know. Well, have a good day."

"You, too, sir." The guard doesn't check my bag. He just let me inside the school premises.

Students greet and walk past me as I go to the faculty and to my desk. My desk is a disaster, with crumpled papers, pens that ran out of ink, and other trash. I threw them on the trash can under my desk. I take the notebooks and put them inside the drawer. I take the laptop from my bag and put it on my desk. I sit and rub my eyes. My class for this day will begin in half an hour.

"Sir Gerry," Alvin said. He's one of the two Entrepreneurship teachers at the school. Unfortunately, his desk is beside mine. "You look like crap."

"Excuse me?"

"Looks like you haven't slept."

"I barely did."

"Working on your student's output, eh?"

"Yeah."

My class goes on as usual. A handful of students amaze me with their developing skill; some persist and still need some assistance; some just continue to piss me off. After my whole day of teaching is done, I call Sarah again and tell her I'm good to go. She tells me to go to a Cafe I never heard of before.

After a few more calls, I arrive at the place she prefers, half the of the chairs are unoccupied. Through the glass doors, I see Sarah leaning forward at the desk on the corner, using her phone, swiping lazily.

"Oh, hi," she says when she sees me approaching. She's beautiful, but the shirt she's wearing doesn't go well with her face. I once had a romantic feeling for her, which immediately dissolved after being closer to her as a friend. Now, we're fine with each other as comrades.

"Your shirt is dreadful." I say as I sit casually across from her.

"Your face is dreadful," she replies in a monotonous voice.

We order Milk Tea for each of us and some fries. She pays for mine. I don't protest because who rejects free foods?

"Because writers are poor," she says matter-of-factly.

"Who said that?" I ask, genuinely curious.

"I don't know. You just strike me as poor."

"Why?"

"You look like a hobo."

"Well, thanks. I make decent money out of my books."

"I read your novella called *When Dogs Fly*."

"How is it?"

"Horrible."

"Well sorry. I tried my best writing that."

"I don't think so," she shifts from her seat. "What's up?"

"Nothing much. Still writing my new book," I say as I take a sip of my Milk Tea. It's horrible. It feels like drinking a child's liquefied poop. I try my best not to grimace. "I named a dog after you."

"No shit?" she says, smiling stupidly.

"Yeah."

"That's nice."

"I killed that dog."

"Damn you."

I chuckle and take another sip, which I regret as soon as the taste hits me again.

"So what's up?"

"I just feel something different lately writing this new novel of mine."

"How different?"

"Well," I say with a low voice, looking to the other people in the cafe like what I'm saying is Classified Information. "I feel afraid of writing. I don't feel excited anymore." I entail what happened last night.

"Oh hell," she says. "You're doing drugs?"

"No. Like I said, I didn't intake anything unusual."

"Maybe you're schizophrenic."

"No. I'm very aware of what was happening. I didn't black out or anything."

"Well, I'm no doctor, so I don't know what's going on with you. But what I know is you could go to a professional and discuss that matter."

"Thanks for listening. I just want to talk to somebody about it. It's been bothering me."

"Don't you think your computer's been hacked or anything?"

"No. It's not typing on its own; my fingers are."

"I mean, your hands couldn't have just quivered and typed random craps," she takes a sip of her drink. It's almost half empty.

"I told you, it's not random crap. There's a story in it. It fits my story, but at the same time, it doesn't."

"I'm sorry, I just couldn't see that being possible. But don't get me wrong. I believe you. Like I said, we could always get some help from someone. It's nothing I've heard before, but it's sure not something unexplainable."

"I don't know."

"Can I look at your work? Maybe you could send me the file via Email."

"No, no. It's okay. Maybe you're right. It should be something explainable." I sip at my drink again, barely minding the horrible taste this time.

"Are you sure you're not just playing a joke on me? Or on yourself?"

"You know that I would never do that."

"Maybe you could just go on and leave it in your first draft. Maybe turn it into a unique writing technique... or something, like a... bug in a code, and you turn it into a feature."

I giggled. "What do you know about programming?"

"None," she said. She's been tracing circles on the table, and I try not to be hypnotized by it. "I just saw a meme. But you know what I mean."

I nodded. "That change in perspective won't be pleasant. And again, it disturbs me. Continuing with it won't be a brilliant idea."

"I'm sorry."

"Nothing to be sorry for. Thanks for listening, anyway."

"My pleasure. And yeah, their Dark Chocolate Milk Tea is disgusting. You shouldn't have ordered that."

"Why didn't you say that earlier?" I'm officially done with my drink. I haven't even drank a quarter of it.

"I just thought it'd be funny."

"You're the evilest person I know."

We chat some more. My writer's life and her teacher's life. We occasionally talk more about what happened, and then return to the fun stuff. I remind her how dog-looking her boyfriend is and I joke that she should just be with me; that we just look better together. She replies *screw you*. We part ways when it's past 6:00 in the afternoon. She reminds me to call her again in case I need to talk to her again.

Talking to her helped a little. It may not have resolved my main problem, but releasing the burden for a while through talking always helps. Sarah is like a clown in the middle of a grim place. Her boyfriend is lucky to have her. Lucky ape.

I decide to walk instead of riding a jeepney to clear my mind. I child beggar comes close to me and asks for a little money. I give him five pesos.

I sweep the surrounding with my eyes; people walking with their phones on their faces, vendors, closing shops, stray dogs, and many more. Being observant of the world around me always helps me as a writer.

Near a Seventh Day Adventist church, there is a group of people in their casual clothes and big bags on their backs. Some of them have towels on their shoulders. It appears to me they're waiting for something. A service vehicle, maybe. Maybe they are relatives going home from a beach or a resort. All of their skins are tan, brown, or light brown. One face, however, stands out. It's like a white pebble on the ground.

The owner of the face has been residing inside the pages of my novel, and most unfortunately, inside my head. What I thought would be my greatest creation became my nightmare. I rub my eyes hard to the point of feeling sore, hoping for the hallucination to be gone. Among those brown faces, the white, dead face is still there. It's definitely not a hallucination.

I try to hold it together. I swallow with an audible gulp and continue to walk fast, almost running. I look behind me and see he's following me. The people around him don't throw a glance at him despite his peculiar looks. A mother with a kid pass by him, but the kid doesn't shout "Look, mommy! That man looks like a dead man!"

Screw it. I sprint.

Once I reach the curb leading to the street where my house is, he's gone.

I stand, shivering, standing at the front of my house. The light in the sky is fading quickly. I take my keychain that holds several keys from my bag with annoyingly clumsy fingers. I insert a key to the hole. Wrong key! I uttered a frustrated sob and tried another key. For a second I think the key won't fit in the keyhole again, but I thanked the heaven for mercy because the door opens. I go inside and lock the door of my house, doubting that the lock will secure it.

I created this man. I know his strength.

But I don't know what's going on in his mind; the deeper, darker part of his mind. I didn't choose to know when I first created him.

I wait for the door to be banged with his big white fist, but no such thing occurs. I examine the windows. All of them are securely locked. With weak legs I go to the kitchen and get myself a glass of water. I wipe the sweat from my face with my cold hand. I go to the living room and sit on the couch. I lean on the backrest and let my head loll back. It takes a while for my breathing to be in control and for the quivering to stop.

I take my phone and think of calling Sarah, but I decide against it.

I go to a window near the door and peek outside. No sign of his dead face; only the neighboring houses, and people outside doing their agenda. The light posts are now on; most of them are powered by solar energy.

I go to my room and lay in my bed without changing my clothes. I contemplate: is it really possible for my creation to be brought to reality? Well, yeah if a studio decides to make a movie adaptation out of my novel. But no, I haven't finished it yet; I didn't even let it be read by someone else already.

Must be another episode of hallucination, I think. A hallucination I don't what caused. It doesn't make a bit of sense.

What if he's actually a real person, I consider. I mean, there is a chance that his image I created in my mind must be accurately similar to someone's here in the real world, isn't there? Maybe I've seen that guy before and my mind somehow retrieved that memory and translated it like it's an original idea. But no, I'm a hundred percent sure that he was created the moment I looked at my dead uncle's pale face, not someone else's.

My heart suddenly pound. Is it uncle? Nah. Nah. It can't be. He's dead. A dead person cannot return to life, right? Well, except Jesus, maybe. But uncle's no Jesus. He's a person, and definitely not a saint.

Like Sarah suggested, I need to meet a professional. A psychologist, a therapist, anyone who can actually help me. I open my laptop and search on the internet and find no office near my place. I search for some more until my eyes close and I doze off. I am not exhausted so I don't know what caused me to sleep.

Chapter 9

I am in a hospital. The details are blurred, but I know to myself it's a Delivery Room. There are two Doctors; one of them is wearing an L.A. Lakers Jersey. In the bed, a woman is giving birth while singing The Beatles' *Penny Lane*, but in some sort of Heavy Metal version. She is not actually shouting while giving birth.

Then a laugh resonates inside the room. It's coming from the woman where the baby is trying to see the world. It's supposed to be a cry, right? But no, it's a laugh. Whatever's coming out of the woman is shrieking with laughter, like a *tiyanak*. Is the woman giving birth to a *tiyanak*?

This is some weird crap, but the weird crap level two started the next moment the woman finishes the first stanza of the song. I am now the one lying in bed. My legs spread open. In the corner of the room, I see myself standing while reading a book. I cannot recognize the title and the author's name, but it's a big book.

"Push," the doctor in the Lakers Jersey, says with a grin.

I do as he says. It almost feels like pooping. Then out of the hole, the man comes out, its dead eyes looking straight at me. The doctors disintegrate into dust. I hear one of them say "I don't wanna go."

The man turns his head from me and walks towards me, the *me* in the corner of the room, now reading a comic book. I try to shout, to warn myself, but instead of "WATCH OUT!" my mouth utters a sound of a chirping crickets.

The man stabs me in the face. I see it all happened.

He turns to me and walks toward me, the *me* that is lying in bed. He readies his knife. His face remains straight, expressionless, lifeless. He opens his mouth and snaps it closed, leaving his teeth bared. It makes a *tak* noise as the rows of his teeth hit each other. He opens his mouth again, then snaps it close again, making another *tak* sound. He repeats this more times until his mouth is making that familiar noise. *Tak-atak-tak-a-tak-tak-tak-tak*.

"No witnesses," he says. His voice sounds like it comes from the pits of hell. *"tak-a-tak-tak-a-tak-a-tak-atak."* He raises his knife and brings it down, and...

Chapter 10

...then I wake up with a shout. I recall what the hell went on in my dream. I've had my share of weird dreams, but this one must be the weirdest. I close my eyes and try to go back to sleep, hoping to wake up in another dream or in no dream at all. Before my consciousness drifts, I hear the sound again, quite clearly.

Tak-a-tak-tak-taka-tak.

Chapter 11

I wake up, my back wet from sweat, leaving an oval shape that's soaking wet on my bed sheet. I get up with a grunt and pee in the bathroom. I wash my face and dry it with a towel.

I go back to my room and take my phone. No new messages. No email. No other notifications.

I prepare breakfast and wolf it down. I didn't realize how hungry I was.

I go out to get some fresh air, and then panic instantly hits me. My heart palpitates. I awkwardly got back inside, hoping no one saw me suddenly jerking, especially not my stalker. I slam the door closed and press my back against it, running my hand through my hair, and thinking, *what if he's just outside, waiting for me?*

I remember my weird-ass dream, especially the giving birth part crap, giving birth to a monster. Disturbing as hell. The act of giving birth alone is unsettling enough, but giving birth to *him*? That's next level. Of course, I know what it implies: I created the monster with my mind, and it's now hunting me for some reason.

I'm still in the stage of denial. A huge part of me still believes that everything that is happening is a hallucination. I gave up figuring out what caused me to see things. There's no other logical explanation, none I can think of, anyway.

Aside from hallucination, paranoia seems to have built up. Maybe it was also a symptom of whatever I consumed. Why did I go back inside after a few seconds of being outside? Why did I run when I saw the man, who only happens to be a hallucination only?

What the devil is going on with me?

I need to change. I need to ignore all of this. I need to finish my novel because readers are eagerly waiting for it. I promised them I'd finish it this year, and I won't be able to do that if I continue to be a damned weakling. I need to finish it. Damn him. Damn the fear. Damn all of this to hell.

I drink a couple of glasses of water and burp.

I get ready for work. I try to focus my mind on teaching and coding. My class ends at noon because of a school event so I get to go home early. With abnormal vigilance I sweep my surroundings with my vision. Up to the point that I get home, there's no sign of a pale face.

Without changing my uniform, I go to my room and plug in my laptop then open it. That light again. That wretched light. I definitely have a loose screw. Who would be afraid of the screen light? Who?

I open the minimized file. I can't remember if I closed the file or not the last time I worked.

The page visible to the screen is my latest progress, the end of the 30th chapter. I proceed to the next page and type CHAPTER 31.

Touching the keyboard brings me uneasiness again, but I have a feeling I'm in control. Everything will be fine. My fingers start typing.

I start with the morning Victor learned of the news. A colleague of his sent him a message and a picture of Richard, his blood already dried in his white shirt. Not far from Richard's corpse is Sarah's carcass, bloodied just like his owner. Gilberto and Pablo arrived at the scene of the crime and his other friends followed. Not long after Richard's relatives followed. There were murmurs and wailing. There were curses and threats. The day went on. There were questionings and other details.

I highlight the whole chapter I finished today and saw the word count. One thousand and Five Hundred Thirty-Nine words. Not bad for a whole day. I am satisfied with a thousand words as my daily quota.

Out of a sense of fiddling, I scroll down the pages of the document, expecting the movement to abruptly stop at the page of my latest progress, but it goes on instead. I don't remember writing anything after writing about Richard's murder. I continue to scroll down, feeling the faint heat caused by the friction of my fingertips against the laptop's touchpad. It shouldn't feel that way, so I conclude it's just another part of my hallucination.

Then I see paragraphs of words. I stop scrolling and stare at them, like staring at a riddle I can't understand. They are alien to me because I didn't write them.

It's not as long as a typical chapter in my novel, but it says what it wants to say.

> *He removed his clothes splattered with blood. Underneath is another shirt with a bible verse printed on it. He balled the bloodied shirt and dumped it in a canal where water was not stagnant. The cloth went with the flow until it disappeared from his view.*
>
> *He's thinking about you. He's got another job, and it is you.*

If he's going to follow whoever the *you*, there's going to be an inconsistency in the story. How's he going to recognize him? How's he going to find him?

> *After a few inquiries with the people around, he finally found the Baranggay you're living in. If you're wondering who's the You, wonder no more. You know to yourself who he is; you just keep denying it.*

No way. My god. Why am I reading this?

> *He wondered around the place, walking under the heat of the sun, his every step's barely making any sound. Despite his peculiar look, he got no turned looks.*

> *Then he saw a familiar face. the face whose eyes have been watching him for a long time. He doesn't want to be looked at funny. He doesn't like the feeling of being watched; that's why he refused to believe in an omnipresent god.*
>
> *Out of a coffee shop you came out with a beautiful woman, maybe your lover. Anyway, she stepped into her car and drove off. You remained standing in that position, looking dumb. He followed you, careful not to get your attention. He stopped behind a group of people with skin complexion different from his. And as if sensing his presence, you turned to his direction. He knew you recognized him because you walked faster than normal. He hesitated at first, then he followed you. He*

I stop reading and close my laptop. Someone was following me. Somehow, he knows how my story goes. Maybe he hacked my computer and looked into my files. Then he followed me through GPS, then did something to his face to make it pale. Then he broke into my house and typed this part of the story.

I suddenly remember the last moments of my dream when the man made a sound from his chattering teeth. *Tak-a-tak-a-tak-tak*. Now I know why it sounds familiar to me. During my sleep, someone was using my laptop and writing that part of the story.

I ready myself to go to the police station. I'm going to report trespassing, or any offense applicable. But I have no proof of intrusion or just evidence of what happened. I didn't notice any marks or dents on my door that shows any sign of forced entry.

The police will only laugh at me like I'm telling a story about dragons and wizards, or maybe shoot me in the face if I happen to talk to one of *those cops*.

No matter. They can call me names or whatever, but I'm going to insist on my conclusion. There's no way I would write those words. I get out of my room and find the main door open. Standing in the doorway... well... is my creation. Behind him is the light from outside, making him look like a shadow. He closes the door, and the sound that it makes reverberates inside my house.

I may not see it, but I know color leaves my face. My chest tightens again and I wet myself a little, eyes are wide open. Almost slipping, I go to my room and lock the door while muttering curses to myself.

It must be my hallucination again, so I shake myself. I briskly rub my eyes with the ball of my palms and slap my face in succession until my cheeks are extremely burning with pain. As I grip the doorknob to confirm my hypothesis, I barely hear footsteps nearing my room; water droplets are loud in comparison.

With a cold voice that seems to come from a pit, he speaks. "It's me."

I don't reply. Another batch of F-bombs escapes my mouth while sweat continues to run down my face. I have a hunch that it will not be impossible right now for me to sweat with blood.

The man knocks on the door softly, as if I'm sleeping inside my room, careful not to startle me. Each tapping sound makes me flinch.

Acceptance of reality suddenly washed over me. Seems like a button in me is pressed and in a moment, I decide that everything that's happening is not part of my hallucination. The idea of a hacker and an intruder dissolve in my mind. Every trace of denials leaves. I know that somehow, he really left the pages of my novel and existed into this world on the hunt for me because I witnessed his crimes, all of it.

He knocks at the door gently again. "Open it." His voice makes it sound like he's whispering right in my ear.

I have no way of defeating him because I created him as a man with a well-defined body. A plea won't stop him because I created him as a psychopath, no feeling of remorse or empathy. He will kill because it's his job. He stomached to kill his own mother, so what am I to him?

Another batch of knocks, this time louder.

I refuse to accept my fate. I will not be killed. How am I going to stop him?

I see my closed laptop. I imagined a floating light bulb above my head just blinked on with hopeful illumination.

He was created because I wrote the novel. What if I deleted everything about him? Will he cease to exist?

I make sure that the door is really locked before I go to my desk with trembling knees. I open my laptop and the page of the document appears on the screen. The knocks on the door become pounding. He's done talking and he's going to bring the door down.

I make my fingers work. There is a resistance in my body's control system, but I fight it with all I have. Even my laptop's against me. The window keeps minimizing on its own, but I keep pressing the keys *alt* and *tab* consecutively to return to the window of the document.

The same time the door opens and splinters of wood and chips of brass fly, I am finally able to press the *ctrl* with my ring finger and the *A* key with my index finger. He looks straight in the eye; his gaze is like a gun pointed at my face. Just like how I made him, there's no life on his face, only the deadness of it. He runs towards me, his knife in his hand, the blade glinting as sunlight hits it.

I press backspace, or smash it instead.

He is suddenly gone. He leaves an afterimage, and not long after it disappears, too. I realize that something else is no more: the product of my hours of work and the dream of publishing it and having it read by people, and even the dream of adapting it into a motion picture.

He took my manuscript with him.

I press the *ctrl* key and S right after, being cautious not to press Z instead. After that, I press *Ctrl* then *F4*.

All of it, gone.

What only remains is the idea. And ideas are cheap if they are not written. In this case, it's better that way. My antagonist's essence will not depend on my ideas alone, that's why he vanished.

Chapter 12

Since that day I have never written anything fictitious. I'm afraid of bringing another devil to this world, or just anyone that's not supposed to exist outside of the world created by my mind.

End

Confession

Chapter 1

Praise God from whom all blessings flow...
His arms were crossed as he sang silently.
Praise Him, all creatures here below...
He would've heard his wife singing beside him; her voice would've been angelic as always, full of love and dedication to the God she served.

Praise Him above, ye heavenly hosts...

By this point, she would've held his hand and squeezed it tightly and his fingers would wrap around it.

Praise Father, Son, and Holy Ghost...

Her head would've been resting on his shoulder.

Amen...

But none of it would happen again, because the Master she had served dutifully and unquestionably, called her home, and left him alone.

The congregation began their murmurs, they shook hands; they asked each other how they were, what's going on in their lives, and what their plans are for the day.

"Brother Joseph."

Joseph turned around and saw Brother Isaiah. He was in his mid-thirties, the same age as him.

"Brother Isaiah. How are you?" He shook his brother's hand. "Great message you gave there."

"All glory be to God," Isaiah said. "It's kind of a complicated doctrine, but God gave me the knowledge."

"Amen," Joseph said quietly.

"How are you doing? How do you cope? It's only been less than a week since you buried her, so it still must be fresh. From time to time, I still feel a pang of pain. Jam had been a good friend for me and my wife and she's like a mother to our kids. We will miss her."

"Thanks. I'm still having a hard time sleeping at night without taking sleeping pills."

Isaiah patted Joseph on the shoulder. "Just make sure you're still taking care of yourself, Joseph. If you need anything, the church is always here for you, and also God. We'll continue to pray for you."

"Yes, yes."

"If you need anything, just call me, alright?"

"I will."

Isaiah left. His wife was outside talking to Mrs. Susan, one of the eldest women in their Church.

Another one approached Joseph, and this time it's Leila, an old, overweight lady. Her eyes were wet and red. She didn't say anything, only pulled Joseph to her and hugged him and patted his back. Joseph hugged her back and said his thanks.

After several hugs, consolation, and offers of company, Joseph managed to get out of the chapel. He saw children chasing each other in their polo, slacks, and ties, while they laughed with glee. He imagined his son or daughter being one of them, but they didn't have any because they couldn't. They had been silent about this issue.

He finally arrived at his car. He opened the door, went inside, and just sat there, staring at the wheel blankly. Then he bit his lower lip and tears flowed freely from his eyes. The same question he had been asking for the past days resonated again inside his mind: *Why?*

He drove home.

He went to his room, and it felt empty as ever. Jam's clothes were gone; her rack of shoes, her small book collection, anything that reminded him of her was either disposed of or given away. The only thing left was a couple of frames hanging on the wall of the room. One was a picture of him and her, both eleven years old. Joseph was wearing a polo with long sleeves and a necktie; Jam was wearing a red dress. They were both Sunday school students. In the second picture, Jam was also wearing a dress, but a white one; Joseph's coat was black. Their smiles were as wide as the one in the first picture.

He sat on his bed. He reached for his Bible and opened it. After a few seconds, he closed it again. He hadn't read it since the passing of his wife.

The way she died was what bothered him. It was just so sudden and so... unacceptable.

While Jam was in a morgue, preparing her for the funeral, Joseph had told his parents-in-law, Mario and

Rita about what he learned from a few witnesses. It was night. Jam was carrying a couple of plastic bags full of groceries. The path she had always taken to head home was flooding. They said the water would reach your ankle. Because of this, Jam took another route: an alley between a closed poultry shop and a clinic. No one saw what had happened to her in the alley. They just found her, bleeding. She was dead when Joseph arrived in the Hospital. She had a major concussion, and as a proof, the right side of her forehead was caved in. There were investigations, and they concluded that it was an accident. The path was slippery with mud and moss, and they saw a mark in the mud; it looked like an elongated sole of a shoe, which matched Jam's. It indicated that Jam had slipped and hit her head in a metal protruding from the wall. They saw huge amounts of blood in that metal, and a few traces of skin, too. Another thing that bothered Joseph is that Jam's wallet was missing. It only means someone had robbed a corpse.

Jam's parents cried hard after he told them everything. Mario hugged the cold body of her daughter and gave her an apology she would never hear. His wife pulled him gently from Jam's corpse and hugged him and told him it's going to be okay, even if it wouldn't be.

Then Mario faced Joseph, fury and sadness were in his eyes; a disturbing mix. "Is this your god?" he said quietly but firmly. "Why her?"

Joseph didn't answer.

Rita told her husband to stop, but Mario went on. "Of all the people, why the one that He considers his 'daughter?'" He grabbed Joseph by the shoulder. "Why?"

"I'm sorry," Joseph managed to say. "I'm as devastated as you are. I'm asking God the same question. I'm still waiting for an answer, and I guess it won't be coming soon."

Mario stared at him, anger started to melt, then he turned and left.

Rita stayed a bit to give his son-in-law a hug and told him God had a plan for everything.

Joseph went to the living room and opened the TV to avert his mind from the sorrow.

Chapter 2

Pastor Jeffrey, a close friend of Joseph and Jam's second cousin, advised Joseph to take a walk outside and get some fresh air and to talk to God. He made dinner for himself, his favorite: skinless longganisa. The way he cooked them was burned, and he thought, if Jam made this, it would be perfectly cooked. He remembered that time when Jam first introduced him to Mario and Rita. She knew it was his favorite, so she cooked it, and it was perfect, and he fell in love more with her.

After he finished his dinner, he washed the dishes. After that, he took a bath, shivering at the cold water.

He went outside, wearing a black jacket. It was a gift from Isaiah.

He walked, thinking of a place where he could be alone with his thoughts and the memory of his wife. Then he remembered the old playground in front of a Catholic school. It was always deserted, especially at night. Kids did not play there anymore; they're always locked in their rooms while their faces were glued on the screen of their cell phones.

When he arrived, he was right: it was deserted. No people nearby, a perfect place to think things over. He sat on a swing and the chain holding it groaned a little, but he knew it's going to support his weight just fine. He swung in small arcs, his feet pinned on the ground, then he got tired and stopped.

Beside him was another swing. It was still. He imagined Jam, the nine-year-old one, in the empty swing, swinging, her small hands holding the rusty chain, and on her wrist a bracelet made of santan flowers that he had made for her.

He suddenly felt the wetness in his eyes and immediately wiped them. He didn't want to cry.

He remembered the first time they met. It was a Sunday afternoon. Rita was a new attendee at their church, and she was holding the hand of a little girl. Rita left Jam on the church playground and told her to behave while she talks with the church members. Little Jam was sitting on the one end of a seesaw, her hands were on the handlebars. The other end of the see saw was raised because no one was sitting there to play with her.

That's when little Joseph stopped playing with his toy car and joined Jam. Joseph reached for the other end of the beam and slowly lowered it. Jam's seat slowly rose until her feet were dangling a few inches from the ground. Joseph sat on the other end, carefully. His hands were on the handlebars, too, and his knees were bent. Slowly, he straightened his legs and Jam's seat slowly descended. No one talked the whole time they played, but one thing was clear between them: they just met each other's best friend.

He heard someone approaching him.

"Sir."

"Go away," Joseph said.

"Sir."

"I said go away, please."

But he did not go away. Instead, he sat at the empty swing beside Joseph.

"Sir, I need to tell you something."

Joseph faced his new companion. It was a boy in a tattered shirt. His face was dark and smeared with dirt but his hair was in fairly good condition.

"What do you want?" Joseph said coldly.

"I know you. You are a church worker. Pastor Joseph."

"I'm not a Pastor."

"Sorry."

"What is it you want to tell me?"

"I'm Justin. Twelve years old."

"I said, what are you going to tell me.?

The boy hesitated. Fear crossed his face, but quickly dissipated. "I listened to a lot of talking mouths here in town."

"What do you mean?"

Justin sighed. "We are homeless, me and my brother. He just turned twenty last week. We've been living in the streets for... about three years. I often walk the town to ask people for change, or leftover food. If not looking for food, I loiter in the streets and listen to people talk, especially tricycle drivers. They talk about interesting stuff."

"Then?" Joseph's brows were raised.

"One afternoon, four days ago, after eating a leftover pizza, I sat on the pavement where the drivers wait for passengers. Most of the time they don't mind me staying there. So I heard what they were talking about: it was about the murdered victim near a clinic."

Joseph swallowed. He fought the urge to ask the kid to don't stop, to continue what he knew, but he remained quiet, listening eagerly to every word uttered, to every detail. He cleared his mind and lent his ears.

"One of the drivers said he saw the victim himself the night it happened. He almost lost his grip by the sight of blood everywhere. He said the victim couldn't have been older than twenty-five years."

Can't blame him, Joseph thought. Jam was thirty-four years old (would've been thirty-five on December), the same age as he, but people often deemed her younger. They would always be shocked to learn that Jam was already in her thirties.

"Others knew who she was. They said she was the wife of the Pastor of a church near the General Hospital. I should've told them you are not a Pastor."

Joseph looked the kid straight in the eye. He wanted to grab the kid by the shirt and shake the information out of him. "Why are you telling me these? "

The kid swallowed this time. Joseph saw his hands clasped together, shaking. His legs were swaying uneasily. When he spoke, his voice was shaking, barely understandable. "Sir, please, please don't hurt me when I tell you. Please don't shout at me."

This made Joseph more eager to hear this boy's story, and somehow more annoyed at him. The night suddenly felt colder and the chirping of crickets sounded louder. "Tell me."

"Please, sir, don't hurt me."

"Tell me," Joseph said while his teeth were clenched together.

"I waited for the police operations to be done. I'm sorry. It was... it was the night of my brother's birthday."

"What date is it?"

"June 23, sir."

That was the night Jam was murdered. The same night he cried at the hospital while kneeling on the cold tiles while several pitying looks were nailed on him.

"We sleep in an improvised tent, made of tarps and metal poles. Every time a storm passes, we have to build a new tent all over again. So that night, I was surprised. My brother brought a whole chicken and a couple of cans of coke. I asked him how he got that. He said someone knew it was his birthday so he gave him money as a gift."

Joseph suddenly knew where that money really came from: from a dead woman, his wife.

"I knew he was lying, but I didn't tell him. It was dawn when I woke up. My brother was gone, probably buying our breakfast. On the layered sheets of cardboard where he sleeps I found a wallet."

Joseph knew what Jam's wallet looked like. "Is it color purple, with a rose embedded in it?"

Justin's eyes grew larger and his mouth opened in a small oblong, and he nodded. "Yes, sir. I looked inside. There was a picture of the murdered woman."

In the picture, Joseph thought, *I am hugging her.*

"You're in it. You're hugging her." Justin paused for a bit and looked like expecting Joseph for a response. When he received none, he continued. "And there were a couple of thousand-peso bills and a few hundreds and a few coins." Justin reached for the back of his shorts and held up the wallet.

Joseph took it with trembling hands. The night felt a lot colder than before.

"My brother doesn't know I took it. He's going to be mad at me. The hundreds are gone. My brother spent them already, I think. Somehow, he kept the picture inside. I don't know why."

Joseph held the wallet in his hands, slightly squeezing it. He opened it and looked at the picture. He pressed his lips together and thawed crystals fell from his eyes again, for the millionth time. He turned away from the kid and quickly wiped his eyes.

"I'm sorry my brother took it."

Joseph nodded. He cleared his throat. "Where do you live?"

The kid told him.

Chapter 3

That night, he prayed, prayed hard.

Chapter 4

The next day went as usual: empty.

He did everything he had to do: clean the house, do the dishes, wash his clothes, continued to make reports for his work, and cried.

That night, he didn't make dinner. He just lay in bed, looking at the ceiling, examining the cracks that looked like branches of a tree. He waited until exactly midnight, then he went out.

There's a burger place he and Jam loved. Whenever Jam was too lazy to make dinner, they would go out and eat burgers there. What Jam loved about them was the double Patty between the buns and the oozing melted cheese.

The vendor knew him and Jam because they'd been regular customers. "Hey, Joseph."

"Hey, Derek" Joseph said, smiling a little.

"I'm sorry about Jam. I'm gonna miss her. She always likes extra onions, you know."

"Yes. Let me get two."

"The usual?"

"Yes."

"Coming right up."

Joseph was trying hard to form the right words to say once he met the thief, but the smell of sizzling beef and the melting cheese kept getting in the way of his thoughts.

After Derek had finished, he gave Joseph the brown bag. When Joseph reached for his wallet, Derek said, "On the house, mate."

Joseph said, "No, no. I insist."

"No, I insist. Please. Let me do this for Jam. She's my friend, too, you know."

Joseph smiled and nodded. "Thank you. I appreciate this. She would love this."

Chapter 5

The tent Justin was talking about was near a waiting shed. The metal poles are attached to each other with straw. The tarp that served as walls and roof had holes and pictures of political candidates.

It's a miracle no one had sent them away yet.

Justine was kneeling over a textbook, coloring a Carabao with a green crayon. Joseph noticed that Justin's right cheek was red and a bit swollen. He imagined Justin's brother slapping him after finding out that the wallet was missing and threw countless curses at him.

His brother was lying in the carton, smoking. He wears no shirt, so his rack of ribs was showing. There was a heart tattoo on his arm.

"Hello," Joseph said. The brothers faced him. Justin was smiling; his big brother was acting confused, but Joseph knew he knew he was in big trouble.

"What?" the older one said and sat up.

"Can I come in?" Joseph said, showing the bag of food he bought. "Dinner."

Reluctantly, the older one nodded.

Justin closed the textbook and moved aside to give Joseph some space to sit on. Joseph opened the bag and gave the brothers each a burger. "My wife loved them," he said.

Slowly, the older brother opened the foil and bit down the burgers. Justin ate heartily. "Why are you here?" Justin's brother asked Joseph.

Joseph gave Justin a look and nodded.

"What?" his brother asked again, his voice trembling.

"Finish your dinner first," Joseph said, smiling, but there was command in his voice.

After they finished, Joseph took out his wallet, and gave Justin a hundred pesos. "What is this, sir?" Justin asked.

"Do you know any store where you can buy coke? The one that comes in cans?"

"There was a convenience store, quite far from here."

"Can you buy some for us? You keep the change."

Justine grinned, stood up, and went out to buy. Joseph watched him leave.

"Hey," the older brother said. Joseph faced him. "Why are you here? Any problem?"

"What's your name?"

The big brother hesitated to answer at first, but answered anyway, "Renato."

"Renato."

"Yes... uh... sir."

Joseph crossed his legs. "Do you know who I am?"

Renato shook his head.

You know me, you lying idiot, Joseph thought. *You saw me in the picture, didn't you?* He took out Jam's wallet and showed it to Renato. "Does this wallet look familiar?"

There was familiar shock on Renato's face. "No," he said, but his eyes said otherwise.

"Do not lie to me, Renato."

"I'm not. Swear."

He opened-closed the wallet, making it move like a butterfly. "Last night, your brother, Justin, found me alone in the playground. I tried to shoo him away, but he stayed, because he had something to tell me."

"I don't—"

Joseph's eyes never left Renato's. "The night of your Birthday, he said you brought a lot food, a little beyond your budget, obviously. Where did you buy that? How did you buy that?"

"Uh..." Renato's eyes were dancing. "There was a... I found five hundred pesos in the street. I used it to buy food for my birthday."

"Your brother said you said it was given."

Renato did not answer.

"Renato, I have no intention of staying here longer. Justin said he found this wallet in there." Joseph pointed at Renato's "bed." "Tell me everything, Renato."

Renato shifted uneasily. "I'm... uhh..."

"Don't leave anything behind, Renato. Why did you take this? Don't worry, I won't tell the police. If you're not asking, I work at a church. We teach forgiveness. I already forgave you for what you did. I just want to know it coming straight from you."

"I told you... I—"

"I know when someone is lying, Renato. I counseled countless young people. I didn't stop until they told me the truth. Now, I'm telling you to spill it all out. I will keep my promise. You will live and take care of your brother. Just tell me, Renato."

Renato attempted to stand up, but Joseph held his shoulders tightly and pushed down. Renato's hands were shaking and his eyes were wet. "Please."

"Renato, I'm not gonna leave until you tell me."

Renato sighed. "I didn't mean to."

"What?"

"I didn't mean to do it. It was... it was an accident."

All air felt to leave Joseph's lungs. "What?"

"I... I asked her, quite nicely, to... give me her wallet. But she ran away. I came after her. I managed to pull her hair."

"What are you talking about?" Joseph's voice sounded different, sounded possessed.

"My sin, sir," Renato said. "I pulled her hair quite hard. She slipped. I heard a loud clang. Then she went down and went still. I panicked when I saw the blood. I searched her bag and took that." He pointed at Jam's wallet. "I'm..." He finally broke down. "I'm sorry. I didn't mean to. I confessed to the priest. I... I always regretted it. I... I prayed... to ask God to... forgive me."

Joseph didn't bother to wipe his wet cheeks. Everything felt crumbling, his life, the world. He imagined the ground swallowing him, and he wanted it to do just that. He wanted to grasp his face, to tear his skin off. He wanted to shout, to shriek for the whole world to hear. He wanted his hands to grasp some neck and choke the life out of someone.

"I'm sorry. Forgive me, sir. I... I'm ready to be imprisoned. I'll surrender myself. I'll always ask God to forgive me. I'll be a... a better man. I'll accept any punishment."

"I forgive you." Joseph said. "I forgive you with all my heart."

"Thank... thank you."

"I'm going to ask you something, Renato. I want you to answer honestly. I want your answer to be true and without hesitation."

Renato regarded him with his wet and red eyes. "What?"

"Do you believe in hell?"

At first, Renato stared at the crying man, his mouth gaping, then he nodded. "Yes... sir. I do, sir."

"Good," Joseph said absently. He stood up and went out of the tent.

On his walk, he encountered Justin. "Sir, there's no coke. I only bought Orange soda."

Joseph ignored the kid and continued to walk. He barely heard the kid calling out to him.

Chapter 6

Rita woke up and looked at the clock: it was two in the morning. She turned to her husband and hugged him, but she grasped air, no sleeping husband. She stood up and went to the living room. There was no sign of him.

These instances weren't new to her. Her husband was a former policeman, and calls on ungodly time were part of the day. But he's retired now, and there's no reason for him to leave, unless there's a reason he didn't want her to know.

Mario had a gun. He was hiding it under the bed, taped to the frame. Rita knew, she didn't just tell him.

She kneeled and looked.

The gun was gone.

Chapter 7

A twenty-year old man was found dead; his body was found floating in the river. There was a bullet hole between his eyes.

The brother he had left was a minor, and was taken care of by an agency that specializes in helping children in need, especially homeless ones.

Chapter 8

It felt good to be behind the pulpit again. It's been a while since Joseph spoke in front of the congregation.

"... it was right that everything happens if God decrees it, even the fall of a leaf from a tree. If God wills you to pass your exam, you will pass. If God wills you to be healed, you will be healed. But remember that these little miracles had to be executed. By what? Of course, by the actions of man. For you to pass, you have to review. For you to be healed, you have to take care of yourself, or let medical workers take care of you. Miracles don't happen without a logical cause..."

The Lord also said "Vengeance is Mine. I will repay. Lord's vengeance does not come without a cause. It also has to be executed. By disease, by calamities, or by the pull of the trigger.

He did not say these. This will kick him out. He saw Mario sitting in the last pew. He smiled at him. *Thanks.*

And Mario smiled back. *You're welcome.*

End

Enclosed

Chapter 1

He woke up. His bed felt... different. It seemed like he wasn't actually in bed.

His cheek was laid against something, and it did not feel like a pillow. A rock, maybe? It was roughly the size of his head. The texture is odd; it's like a dried fruit peel or a wafer. Whatever it was, it's not a comfortable pillow, but at least its coldness compensated for it.

He figured out he was lying down on his belly, but what he couldn't figure out was what kind plank his body rested upon; it was narrow; his body barely fitted on it. There was also a slight softness to it, like an old long cushion. In his arms he could feel its rough bed sheet.

He opened his eyes. Panic instantly hit him. His vision was pitch-black.

He tried to stand up, but his back hit something, like a glass, and it forced him to return to his previous position. He tried to stretch his arms, but was abruptly stopped when his hands reached the wall on his either side that felt like covered with a thin cushion.

He knew he was enclosed inside something.

He was able to bend his arms and wipe his sleepy eyes with his hand. He touched the sides of his cold, hard pillow. Something was protruding, like a...

Like a nose.

There were other crevices that he felt. He moved his hands more around the 'pillow', and he felt something, like fur... or hair.

Realization washed over him.

He screamed. He wiggled his limbs frantically. Again he attempted to stand up, but his back met the glass casing again. He closed his hands, his nails digging in his palms, and rapped at the walls on his sides; it made a hollow sound.

The comforting coldness of his pillow was gone. The cold was now eerie, strange, and disturbing. He felt like his cheek would freeze and half of his face would be numb and paralyzed.

He crawled backwards until his cheek left his cold 'pillow'. He stopped when his feet reached the end of the 'box'. He kicked at it, but just like before, the hitting sound was not reassuring, instead, it told him that there's no way he's coming out of here.

He attempted to roll his body to be able to lay on his back, but his shoulders hit the glass. He squeezed his body, squashing part of his 'bed' in the process. He could feel and hear a few 'twigs' snapping. But his efforts were unsuccessful. He remained in his dreadful position, but least his face was off that 'pillow'.

Resting his head on the rough fabric of Barong Tagalog was less bad.

"HELP!" he shouted. "SOMEBODY!"

But he imagined himself several feet below the surface. Who could possibly hear him beside his odd 'bed'?

He remained still. He had watched a few of George A. Romero's movies, and that memory definitely didn't help. He expected the arms to close around him anytime. He expected a groan from his 'pillow', or a chuckle, or a shriek, or just plain *how ya doin'?*

It shrieked; its sound was digging painfully in his ears.

But it didn't. It was his mind playing tricks on him.

Now he felt something in his legs. Something moved, making his leg rise a few inches. Again, it might just be his mind. Same case with the hands that brushed his arms and the rustle of the hair.

His trembling worsened. His face dripped with more sweat. His clothes stuck to his soaking body. His windpipe seemed to close; he couldn't breathe. He closed his eyes and urged himself to relax. His breathing became okay. Once he felt slightly fine, he moved his head to the side and retched, then his breakfast came out of his mouth. His body convulsed painfully and his throat felt sore. He heard the splashing sound, which made him want to throw up more. And because of his dire state, he could smell his own puke. There was still a faint trace of Adobo. "Sorry," he muttered.

He wiped his face. He hadn't realized he was crying. He had never cried before because of fear.

A question suddenly popped into his mind: How did I get here?

The answer followed immediately.

Chapter 2

He was sitting on one of the four benches near a mall, a brown envelope in his hands. Inside it was a two-page document detailing his personal info. He took it out and checked the filled-out form. His name was in correct spelling; his birthday was correct; same with his address, contact number, email address, and other weird craps he had had to fill up.

Beside him, an old man sat. His hair was gray and long. His shirt and shorts were streaked with dirt. His skin was dark and there were some black spots on it.

"Good morning," the beggar said.

Patrick didn't answer. He moved several inches away from the old man and looked at him with disgust, not trying to hide it.

"It's a nice day," the old man said. In his hands was a paper covered in plastic. Patrick looked at it and realized it was a form, the same one he had answered. He saw the name. It was Anton.

"Anton?"

"Yes?" The old man turned to him with slight curiosity.

"Where did you get that?"

"What?"

"That form." Patrick pointed to the man's paper.

"Oh, this is a job offer. I'm meeting with the boss. They said the pay is huge. They showed me the other benefits. I could finally provide for my family. We are tired of living under the bridge."

"Weren't you skeptical about it?" Again, Patrick pointed to the paper. "I mean, obviously, you're a beggar. Why would they offer you a job? Why would you be qualified?"

Anton looked a bit hurt. "They said they don't need anyone with a college degree. What they need is someone who can do heavy works. I mean, I'm old, but I still could do work. After I lost my job as a school guard, it wasn't long before we became broke, then soon after we were forced to live under the bridge. I do construction, but it's not regular, so the pay isn't always enough."

"Did they show you any papers or what to show that they're legit?"

"Yes. I looked at the papers, although not thoroughly. Still, I'm convinced. Why do you ask?"

"I got the same offer." He showed Anton his form. "They didn't say what kind of work it was; they insist on not telling me. But they assured me it's legal. They told me it's physical work. I have no health issues. As you can see, I am in perfect shape despite my age."

Anton nodded, impressed. "Well, looking forward to working with you."

"Yeah," Patrick said. "Whatever. What else did they tell you?"

"They told me to wait in this very spot. A black sedan will pick us up."

"Hell. Guess we're really working together."

Minutes later, the car arrived. A bald man in a black suit came out of the car and shook Patrick and Anton's hands. "Sirs," he said. His eyes were small and his nose was huge. That made him look like a cartoon character, like the goofy and idiot apprentice of a hot-headed, short character.

"Are you the one from WillCruz Corp.?" Patrick asked.

"Indeed, sir," the bald man said. "I believe you two are Patrick Guillermo and Anton Santiago."

They nodded.

"I am told to pick you up today. Please, get inside. We'll have a long ride ahead."

Patrick took his bag and envelope and went inside. Anton brought nothing except the form. They sat beside each other at the backseat while bald man on the driver's seat.

"Ready, sirs?"

"Yes," Patrick said. "We're ready to go."

The bald man pressed a button and a glass rolled down between the driver's seat and the backseat. There was a humming sound, which abruptly stopped as the glass completely rolled down.

"Hey," Anton said. "What's this?"

"Just for my safety, sir," the bald man said.

"What the—" Anton turned to Patrick. "Can you believe it? What the hell does he think we are?"

"Just shut up," Patrick said irritably. "What's the big deal with it? Stop fussing about it, you big baby." He crossed his arms and leaned his head against the window. "Stupid idiot won't stop bitching about the whole ride," he muttered to himself.

"Well, I changed my mind. I'm not looking forward to working with you. You're kind of a schmuck."

"Just imagine how Mr. Driver here feels about you."

"It's okay, sir Guillermo," Mr. Driver said. "And you can call me Javier." Javier pressed another button.

"Now what?" Anton said.

Gas filled the backseat. Patrick, who had been closing his eyes to try to sleep, continued to slumber. Anton screamed for help and tried to open the door, but he found that it was locked. When the gas completely filled his lungs, he fell sideways. His head ended up on Patrick's shoulder.

Chapter 3

Patrick aroused, his throat feeling dusty.

He was sitting in a chair. His arms rested on the armchair with leather cushion. He studied the room he was in; it's a typical office. There were bookshelves, file cabinets, a mini bar, and desks. In front of him was a large desk, and on it were a few pens, papers, and other office stuff.

He tried to stand up, but his body appeared to be glued to the chair.

His back was on the door, and he heard it open. A tall man in his fifties with a cigarette in his mouth entered the room. His hair was slicked back. "Good day, sir Guillermo," the man said and sat down behind the desk.

"What the hell is with this chair?" Patrick said. "I can't get up."

The man blew a cloud of smoke. "There's nothing wrong with the chair, Mr. Guillermo. Your body's the one that's got a problem."

He was right. Patrick couldn't move a muscle, and he felt no resistance caused by being glued or stapled to something. He was only able to move his neck. The rest of his body was paralyzed. "What the hell did you do to me?"

"Our doctors just injected something into you. Don't worry, it's not deadly. You will be able to move your body in the next 5 hours or so."

"Why am I here? Who are you?"

"I am the head of WillCruz corp. You were offered a job, I believe."

"Yes. And I should be in an interview right now. As far as I'm concerned, rendering me immovable shouldn't be a part of my application, so what the hell?"

The man stubbed his smoke into the ashtray. "Please, sir, tell me everything you know."

"About what?"

The man shrugged. "About this—" he made air quotes— "job offer."

Now Patrick was a hundred percent sure something was off. "Well, a man from WillCruzcorp interviewed me regarding my financial status because he saw me in an eatery washing dishes because I couldn't pay for the food. I told him that my total money is less than five thousand pesos. I was just fired from my job because of misconduct. I told him it wouldn't be long before I live in the streets, so he offered me a job that does not require a college degree." If he could move, he would've shrugged. "I was desperate."

"So, you're desperate and in need of a job. Any kind of job."

"Of course, a legal one. The guy showed me the papers and my verdict is that the company's legit."

The man put his feet on the top of the table and crossed his arms. "I have a confession to make, Mr. Guillermo: there's no job."

"What?"

"You heard me. There's no job. There'd be no interview, no application. You won't hear 'you're hired.' There's no WillCruz corp. I only made that up."

"Then why am I here?" Fear made his eyes widen. "God, please, don't hurt me. I didn't do anything wrong." His face contorted with an effort to move, but his body remained unresponsive. 'Please, please."

The man only smiled at him. There was pity in his eyes. "Mr. Guillermo. Please tell me what happened on... um... March 23, 2017."

"What?"

"March 23, 2017."

"I... I can't remember. What's this all about?"

"You can't remember?"

"I can't. Will you just please let me go?" Sweat ran down from his forehead. "Please."

The man removed his feet from the table. From a drawer, he took a few stapled papers. He read it and looked at Patrick amusingly. "Isn't it a bit odd that an application form would include something about phobia, among other unusual questions? Well, of course, it's a job application. You were obliged to fill out the form, however odd it may seem. If the form asked you how many times you touch yourself every week, your desperation to get a job would make you answer honestly, right?"

Patrick didn't answer.

"According to Mr. Santiago's paper, he's arachnophobic, meaning he's afraid of spiders." The man chuckled. "I once had a friend who loses his crap whenever he sees a spider."

"Where did you take him? Anton, I mean."

"He's not of your concern. You won't hear his annoying voice anymore because his mouth would probably be filled with... spiders."

The hairs on Patrick's nape and arms stood. Just thinking of the idea would have made his whole-body shiver.

"And you..." The man grinned. "You have... huh... interesting. It says here that you are irrationally afraid of corpses, coffins, funerals, cemeteries... basically anything associated with death. In other words, you have what we call *Necrophobia*."

Patrick lost his strength to answer. He had a funny feeling in his crotch, the one usually caused by fear or distress. He had a clue what would happen to him. Anton was afraid of spiders, and now his mouth was full of them.

"Is it right, sir? Or am I wrong?"

Patrick shouted as he started to cry. His neck moved sideward and shook his head briskly, but his body remained completely still. "PLEASE GOD NO NO NO!"

The man crumpled the paper and threw it across the room. Patrick's eyes weren't able to follow its course in the air. "Three points!"

"Please don't don't! I did nothing wrong!"

"Let me give you a clue." The man stood up and put his hands in the pockets of his pants. He paced the room leisurely. "Mr. Santiago's afraid of Spiders. We put him in a room full of those little guys. I'm gonna be honest with you; the shrieks of the men I punish kind of disturb me. So I made my men make the walls a bit special. Anton could shout his lungs off, but we won't hear a thing. The spiders won't be scared by his shout. They will crawl upon his skin. They might even bite. I could almost feel them in my own skin just thinking of them." He trembled on purpose and mockingly.

Patrick's wet face contorted once more, but he still made no progress. "Let me go! I'll kill you!"

"Mr. Guillermo, it amuses me that you still have the guts to throw threats at me. I mean, look at the both of us."

"I'll—"

"You obviously don't know why I'm going to do this. Do you know anyone named Oliver?"

"No."

"Remember the date I told you? March 23, 2017. Honestly, I wouldn't blame you if you couldn't remember anything. It was the day before the birthday of a kid named Russel." The man leaned at a shelf; he stretched his leg and crossed his arms.

"Russel's parents promised him of a clown for his birthday. The kid was thrilled, I mean, who wouldn't be? Everybody loves clowns for their birthday, right? So he waited for his birthday, and that day came, March 24th; the clown did not come. They found out that he had a serious concussion and had to be admitted to the hospital and had no time to inform Russel's parents that he won't make it. This made the kid go berserk. I can't blame him. Even I would throw a tantrum if that happened to me. During that fit of his, he hit his head in the corner of a metal gate." The man put his hands inside the pocket of his pants. "Guess, did Russel survive that injury or not?"

Patrick only looked at him and snarled at him.

"Heh. I love it when they do that. Anyway, the kid died. The trauma was too much. His parents were wrecked. The mother almost killed herself." The man walked across the desk to a small ref. He took a bottle of water and drank, not offering any to Patrick. "They asked me for help. Of course, I helped them. Do you know why? Because that kid is my Grandson."

"Oh. I'm sorry." Patrick was calm now.

The man waved his hand as if Patrick had just told a joke. "Now, back to my previous question, do you know anyone named Oliver?"

"No."

"Here's a clue. Aside from his profession as an entertainer clown, he's also working at a convenience store."

Memories rushed in Patrick. Everything was clear now.

The man seemed to notice his realization. "And I guess you just understood everything. I will not fill in the details." He looked over Patrick's sholder, raised his hands a bit, and nodded. "I also won't tell you where they'll take you or if you'll live. I always prefer giving people surprises. But I guess you already have a clue."

Again Patrick pleaded, but again, it fell on deaf ears.

"You may be thinking, what's with the WillCruzbullcrap? Well, I love to give you guys a bit of hope that your life would be better when it's the exact opposite. I don't even know who the hell Will Cruz is."

Huge hands grabbed Patrick's shoulder.

"And as for Anton, he has a different story. He shouldn't have let his worldly desires get the better of him." The man laughed. "I actually was tempted to cut his thing off."

Chapter 4

He could already feel the lack of adequate air.

He thought of Anton. If he could just switch places with him that would be completely fine. Patrick was never bothered by Spiders. He would calmly squash one when he saw one. Now, he wondered if Anton was still alive. He wondered how did it feel, thousand tiny legs crawling on your skin, and some going down your throat like Santa as he goes down the chimney.

He had managed to calm himself, but his heart never ceased its rapid beating. He'd prefer it if it would beat until it explodes to make things go faster. He didn't want to stay in this situation.

He had planned of opening his own business once he saved enough money from this work. But there's no work. There'd be no money; only fear and certain death.

I wanna die, he kept repeating in his mind. There's obviously no getting out of this. Once people find out, he would probably be cold and lifeless like Pedro here.

Yes, he named his current companion Pedro. He guessed that Pedro had just been buried recently.

Maybe less than a couple of weeks. The man in the office really chose a fresh body.

The fools had no respect for the dead.

It smelled so bad (he wondered why he hadn't noticed it before), but not to the point of causing nausea. He imagined if the smell had reached its peak, he'd probably die. Good thing? No. It's a nasty way to die.

He tested if he could swallow his tongue. No good.

He attempted to sleep, but Pedro's face kept flashing in his mind. It's a blessing that it was dark inside. He wouldn't bear the sight of Pedro's ashen and wilting face; his pale hands and dark nails; no, he would have none of it.

He had prayed, but hopelessness was just too much for him.

I'd die with dread as my friend.

Heh. It rhymes.

When will it be over? I want it to be over, Oliver.

Oliver.

That was your name, you dope.

Why did we have to meet, Oliver? Why?

God, please kill me now. You can send me to hell or whatever. Just get me out of here.

Chapter 5

He was confident that he's going to win. He was planning to buy a new phone with the money. The one he was using was not charging. The charger was still new, so he had been sure that the problem was with his phone. Having it repaired crossed his mind, but his phone was like a person with a terminal illness. It won't be long before it gives up.

He lost badly. He just shook his head as the other players counted the wad of money they had won. The corners of their smiling mouths almost reached their ears. They were laughing and throwing jeers at the big loser of the night.

"You should've heard yourself before we started," a player said. His feet were on the table. In his hand was a half-empty bottle of beer. "You were very confident you'd take our money, weren't you?"

Patrick didn't answer.

The man with the beer mimicked Patrick; the corners of his mouth were pulled down, and he distorted his voice to make the imitation funnier. He comically swayed his head sideward for added effect. "'Imma take all yer money... yergonna go home poor.'"

Another player, a man with long hair and a pot belly, laughed. His voice was raspy. "That's a good one."

"Just stop," Patrick said.

"Well, I'm sorry. Guess there's no new phone for you." He threw a couple of cards at Patrick.

The cards hit Patrick lightly and the nine of hearts fell on his lap. "I'm going home." He stood up. Seeing his money at the hands of the other players pained him. All the hours of work were for nothing. He felt like he worked, and these players got his salary.

He flipped the bird at all of them and they laughed and taunted him more. He went out of that place burning with rage. He was mad at the boneheads who had his money and he was mad at himself for being so damn stupid. He walked with that burden on his head.

He arrived at a convenience store. He went in and heard a bell above his head. The ringing irritated him. He wanted to yank it out and throw it at whoever put the wretched thing there.

He proceeded to the aisle where the refrigerators for drinks were placed. He opened one of them, randomly took a bottle and brought it to the cashier, placing the sweating bottle at the counter. He took his wallet and almost broke down at what was left inside. He felt like he was robbed. He took the remaining bill and handed it to the cashier.

"Um... you're twenty pesos short." The cashier was a young man whose chin was longer than normal.

"What?" Patrick said irritably.

"You're twenty pesos short."

"So?" He wasn't drunk, but he wanted to be.

"You have to pay in full."

Patrick urged himself not to gouge out that set of smug eyes. "Look. I lost a lot of money. Can't we just let this slide? It was only twenty pesos."

"Well, you said it yourself. It's just twenty pesos. If that's not big money for you, then pay it," the cashier looked at him, trying to match his burning gaze, but he didn't last long. He averted his eyes and blinked. "Look, I'm sorry. I can't. Just return when you already have enough money. There's no bargaining here. You always pay the right price."

"Right price?"

"Right price."

Patrick grabbed the neck of the bottle and a second later shards were flying. Cold beer splattered at the counter, at the walls, the floor, and at his face. The sprinkle of cold liquid was somehow refreshing. The young cashier had gone sprawled on the floor, a few boxes of condoms and chewing gums surrounded him.

Patrick examined him, fearing that he had killed him. Blood was oozing from the cashier's head, but Patrick could see his chest rising and falling. He left the convenience store with a new cold bottle of beer in his hand.

His body was shaking.

Chapter 6

He thought he was gonna last a day.

No.

His fear was still there. He was inside a thing he feared, and with him another thing he feared with his whole life. After the first one, he'd puke two more times. The third time barely let out anything.

He'd tried his best not to touch Pedro's hands. Every time his warm hands would touch the cold ones, shivers would be sent throughout his body and profanities would automatically come out of him. *You kiss your mother with that mouth?* Pedro asked.

He prayed again.

He didn't have the strength to shout or to slam his fist against the wall of the 'box'. His legs were barely movable. He felt like he was paralyzed once again.

He was also extremely thirsty.

When he had felt the warning of suffocation, he knew it wouldn't be long before air left him. He imagined his lungs would be like dried soil, which would easily crumble at the grasp of a hand.

He licked his cracked lips and prayed once more.

Half an hour later, his prayer was answered.

His last thought had been Anton. He had wondered what atrocity the old man had done.

End

Freebie

Chapter 1

"He's like my mother's best friend," Angelo said to his girlfriend, Alexandra. "Whenever my mom was bullied when she was a child, Tito Gordon would kick those bullies in the ass, literally. The unlucky ones would be kicked in the private parts." He chuckled.

"If I'm not mistaken," Alexandra said as she traced spirals on the window of the bus with her finger, "your Tito Gordon is your mother's second cousin, right?"

"First, actually. Tito Gordon is the youngest son of Lola Estella. Lola Estella is the eldest sister of Lolo Julio, my mother's dad."

"Your Tito's kind enough to let us stay in his place for a while."

"Yeah, very. He's the best uncle I have. Once, my father had an accident on the day of my graduation. He had to go to a hospital and my mother had to take care of him, so from here, Tito went to us. He walked me to the stage. And after that, we went to the mall. He bought me toys and stuff. I was embarrassed because I didn't have any awards, but he said that finishing elementary was a reward in itself." Angelo paused for a while. "When my father died four or five years after that graduation, Tito Gordon shouldered half of the funeral expenses. Well, my father and Tito were best friends, so it's not really surprising."

The bus came to a stop and a passenger with his daughter walked down the aisle. Once they got out, the bus went on.

"Are you excited?" Angelo asked and smiled at Alexandra.

Alexandra leaned her head to his shoulder. "Very. Mama said it's a bit impractical that we have to travel hours to get to a good beach when there are decent resorts nearby."

"Well, it's not as good as the one we're going to. They got a lot of exciting gimmicks there. You could ride a Banana boat, or... um..."

"Or...?"

"I don't know anything else, but there are more. I just forgot."

"Yeah, I know. I saw the brochure."

"Thank the heavens your parents let you go alone with me."

"They trust you. And they trust me, of course. What does your mother have to say about this?"

"She's okay with this as long as I keep myself... ourselves from doing something we'll, you know, regret."

"Okay."

When they reached their destination, the bus stopped and they went out, carrying their bags full of clothes and other things. They rode a tricycle until they arrived at a house surrounded by many trees, like a cabin in the woods. They could hear the chirping of birds, the rustling of leaves, and the distant sounds of motorcycles and tricycles.

"This is a lovely place," Alexandra said. "Full of fresh air."

"Yeah. You see that tree?" He pointed to the one near the house. "I used to climb that when I was a kid every time we visited Tito here. I fell once and broke something."

Alexandra let out a restrained laugh. "That's what you get when you have too much coke."

"Right. Sugar always gets in my system."

Alexandra sighed.

They went to the house and Angelo knocked on the door and called "Tito!" No one answered. He knocked and called again, but still no response.

"Maybe he went out or something," Alexandra said.

"Yeah. Probably. Let's just wait under that tree."

They sat on a long, wooden plank nailed to two trees. The plank creaked alarmingly, and they abruptly stood up as if they had sat on a needle.

"It won't support our weight," Angelo said. "You're too heavy."

Alexandra punched him in his arm.

"Wait," he said. "I'm gonna text Mama. I'll tell her we arrived." Then he did.

About ten minutes later, a tricycle came; its tires were crunching dry leaves on the ground. A pudgy man wearing a *sando* and a *maong shorts* stepped out of the sidecar. He had thin hair, big nose, and rosy cheeks. His neck was almost non-existent. He looked like Santa Claus, but retired. He was carrying a jacket and a cap in a plastic bag in one hand, on the other was a box that looked like the box of a mug.

"Angel!" The man cheerily called, and the tricycle left after he gave fifteen pesos to the driver. "How are you?"

Angelo jogged toward his uncle. Gordon put the plastic bag under his arm to let his nephew do the *mano*. "We're good. How are you doing, Tito?"

"Good, good. Still alone in life, but I guess not, temporarily. How long will you stay here?"

"Just three to four days, Tito."

"Oh, that's nice. Who's the beautiful gal?" Gordon nodded his head toward Alexandra.

"Um... she's Alex, my girlfriend."

"Hi!" Gordon said, smiling and waving. To Alexandra, he looked like a human Teddy bear.

"Hi, Tito." Alexandra went to Gordon and put his knuckles on her forehead.

"Angel's such a lucky guy to have you," Gordon said, then punched Angelo slightly in the shoulder.

Alexandra averted her gaze from the human Teddy bear and colors rose to her face. She's not used to compliments when it comes to her physical beauty.

"Where've you been, Tito?" Angelo asked.

"The thrift store. I'm going out with my friends next week and I need something to wear because it'd be cold there, they said."

"What's in the box? Mug?"

"It's a freebie. It comes with the jacket. It's like a little statue made out of porcelain or something else, I'm not sure. Come, let's go inside. The sun's getting higher. It'd be a shame if something happens to your smooth skin." He took the key from the back of his shorts, slid it into the hole, turned it, and opened the door. "Come in, come in."

The two followed with their bags in their hands.

"Why did he call you 'Angel?'" Alex whispered to Angel, careful not to be heard by Tito Gordon.

"Um..."

She didn't do a good job because Gordon said, "Why, you ask?" He faced the two, grinning at his nephew. "Didn't he tell you his nickname?"

Alexandra scratched her arm that wasn't itching. "He told me he's called Gelo—"

Gordon threw back his head and laughed. "You little liar," he pointed at his nephew.

Angel smiled; it was time for his face to turn red. "Just put your bags there," Gordon pointed at the long wooden chair, "and take a rest. I'll be making lunch. Alexandra, I hope you're not allergic to any seafood."

"No, Tito. Maybe I can help with—"

"No nono. You guys take a rest while I cook. It won't take long," then Gordon disappeared into the kitchen.

Alex and Angel took off their shoes and put it outside together with Tito Gordon's shabby slippers. Then they sat, leaning against each other.

"Tito Gordon cooks the best sisig in the world," Angel said. "And once you taste his Carbonara, it'll ruin any other pasta dishes for you."

"Really?" Alex replied lazily.

"Yes. Italian dishes are not his forte, but his recipes are amazing. The only one better than him when it comes to pasta is Lola Pora. She's in Visayas."

"Uh-huh."

"All this talking makes me hungry. Are you starving already?"

"A little bit," she paused, then smirked, "Angel."

"Stop that. It's not uncommon for men to be named 'Angel.'"

"Yeah, sure. Angel."

Chapter 2

The house was just your typical *probinsiya* house. The walls were not painted, but the texture was smooth. The furniture was arranged quite pleasantly. Overall, the house was not that big, but it's enough for... well... three occupants.

Alexandra was dozing off when she smelled the familiar sour and savory scent. "Oh my god, that smell..."

"I told you. He can make Wolfgang Puck drool."

"Who's that? He's a musician, right?"

Tito Gordon cooked *Sinigang na Hipon*. They ate heartily. The cook was pleased to see his food being wolfed down by his visitors.

"Isn't it a bit salty?" Gordon said, trying to sound worried, but in fact, he had a lot of confidence in himself when it comes to cooking. He knew very well that his *sinigang* was perfect. Gordon Ramsay would totally lose his marbles once he gets a taste of this. Gordon often jokes with his relatives that Gordon Ramsay was named after him. When one of them would say "he's older than you," he would reply "You're just jealous."

"I think it's great," Alex said, then sucked the juices from a shrimp's head.

"Yeah," Angel said. "I'll never have enough of this soup."

The compliments are music to his ears. "By the way, where do you guys plan to go?"

"Well, we're going to the beach tomorrow," Angel answered. "Then the day after that, we'll go to the mall. Then spend a whole day here to rest before we return to Manila."

"Oh... yeah." Gordon slurped some of the sour soup straight from a separate bowl beside his plate. "The beach here is great. The cottages are exceptional, but also not that expensive. There's also a lot of food bars there, and they are affordable."

"Yeah. We chose the right one."

"Um..." Alex said, "maybe you could join us, you know. So that... um... you, too, could have fun."

"Oh, really?" Gordon's face brightened even more. "I would love that! Sure, I'll come with you two. We'll have fun!"

Alex and Angel chuckled awkwardly and gave each other a look that said *Oh crap*.

"HA! Just kidding! Of course, I won't come with you. You kids just enjoy your moment. Besides, I got work tomorrow."

Relief washed over them, but they did not show it.

"The last thing you'd want is a vacation ruined by a boomer," a few grains of wet rice flew from Gordon's mouth, but he didn't seem to notice it.

The two were not hungry anymore.

Chapter 3

Gordon showed them a room. Inside it was a big bed made of bamboo with a white mattress on it. There were also four pillows and a couple of folded blankets. Beside the bed was a drawer. On the wall to the left of the bed was a window. Beside it was an oval mirror.

"Well, it's not much," Gordon said, scratching his butt, "but I hope it will do you just fine."

"About that," said Angelo, "I think I'll just sleep on the long chair."

"Why?" Gordon was frowning. He looked at Alexandra; she was studying her feet as though there's something fascinating about them. "Oh."

"Yeah. It's improper for us to sleep in... you know... in the same room."

"You're right. I never thought of that," now he's scratching the back of his head. "Okay. Guess your parents taught you well."

None of the two replied to the compliment; they just smiled at each other.

"You guys take a nap or something. I'll go to my room and sleep for a few hours, as I always do."

After Gordon left, Alexandra laughed silently, then pinched her nose with her fingers.

"What?" Angel asked, smiling a little.

"Didn't you smell that?" she said, still giggling. "He farted."

Angel sighed. "You always find a way to make fun of som—oh god!" He smelled it, too, and like his girlfriend, he pinched his nose.

Alex put her hand to his boyfriend's shoulder. "I have a confession to make," she said with a seriousness Angel had hardly heard before. She wasn't laughing anymore.

"What?" he said, a bit nervous.

"It was me," the seriousness in her face broke, then she laughed again.

"Oh, god. Your fart's the worst; worse than my mom's."

"But you still love me, right?"

"Of course, I love you and your atomic fart."

"Do you think he smelled?"

"I hope so."

Then they laughed hard again, slapping each other.

Chapter 4

There was something strange during dinner. It was in the air.

Tito Gordon cooked *Pancit Canton*. It filled half the pot.

"You know, Canton is actually better without rice."

"Yeah," Angelo's focus was not on the food but on the seven-inch statue that was on the table. It stood beside Tito Gordon's glass of cold water. It's pretty unusual for someone to put a toy, or a statue on the table while eating. There was something wrong with that figurine, he thought. Something disturbing and menacing. Its steady gaze made him uncomfortable. He had been trying his best not to look at it while eating, but it always seemed to call his attention. *Psst. Hey. Yeah, you. How's the food? Did you know it's fatal to eat that at night? Your pancreas will expand, then you will have a nightmare. I'll be in it. Then you'll die. Sounds lovely, doesn't it?*

He looked at his girlfriend. She did not appear to be bothered by the little guy, but if she was, she's doing a good job not showing it.

"I was supposed to buy some *pandesal*," Gordon said, his mouth half-full with the food, "it really goes well with this." There were several dancing strands of Pancit hanging from his mouth, like tapeworms. He sucked those to his mouth with a sloppy sound that made the two wince a little. His lips were greasy.

Angelo never saw his uncle like this... disgusting.

The two remained silent. They hardly put Pancit in their mouths. Their heads were bent to their plates, as if examining the food for worms or something. They couldn't look at Tito Gordon. There was something with him and his new toy.

The pudgy man broke the awkward silence when he said "this new toy of mine, at first look, I didn't want it. It looks funny and it looks at me funny. But then Freddy, the owner of the shop, said that it comes with the jacket, free of charge. When I heard that, my mind suddenly changed. *I want it,* I thought to myself."

Angel was surprised to hear Alex talk for the sake of being polite," It looks nice. It's... uh... cute."

The cute figurine she was talking about looked like a saint. It was wearing a green robe with an inverted star printed on it. Angelo swore that he saw that symbol somewhere else; maybe in a band, he was not sure. It had long brown hair; its beard and mustache were long, too; its fully-black irises were eerily expanded; and it's not smiling; it's smirking, like Mona Lisa.

"Yep, it is," Gordon took his glass of water and drank clumsily; streams of water flowed from the corners of his mouth, soaking his blue t-shirt. "Ahh.

It is beautiful. It's like everything you could ever wish for." He put his two fingers together, put them on his mouth, then touched the head of the figurine with them. "Everything."

Angelo couldn't take the feeling anymore. He faced his uncle and asked, "are you okay, Tito?"

Gordon burped then looked at him, making him more uncomfortable.

Angel felt Alex touch his arm. *Please, just stop talking. There's obviously something wrong with him.* But he ignored her. "I don't know. You act a bit... uncoordinated." From the beginning of their meal, Angelo knew that Gordon was uncoordinated; the way he held the fork looked very similar to the way a baby would hold it; he also seemed oblivious of the falling short strands of *Pancit* on the floor (there were some sticking to his shirt). He acted like a one-year-old feeding himself, but the couple had remained silent about it, until now.

"Uncoordinated?" Gordon wiped his mouth with the back of his hand.

"Maybe you need some rest, or something. Alex and I will do the dishe—AH!" He hadn't realized this until now; he hadn't been looking at his uncle while he talked; he was looking at the small figurine. And it winked at him.

Alex put a hand on his shoulder, her face alarmed. "Why, what's wrong?"

Angel faced Alex and tried to talk, but no word came out. He just looked her straight in the eye; both sets were widened. Tito Gordon, meanwhile, only stared at them with complete disinterest in his face, like a kid watching the clouds in the sky drift.

"Uh..." Gordon said, "I... I will sleep. You guys take care of the dishes." He stood up from his seat slowly and awkwardly, not taking his gaze away from the two.

"Yes, Tito." Alex said, frowning at the odd way Gordon was standing: right elbow slightly raised and his head was leaning on it. "We'll take care of this. You go now and take a rest."

Gordon stared at her, his mouth slightly open. Then, slowly he reached for his toy and quickly tucked it under his shirt; it bulged beneath it. "Good night, lovebirds." He nodded then turned away from them and walked toward his room.

Alex sighed with relief when the figurine (and Tito Gordon) was out of sight. "Hey," she touched Angel's cheek. "Are you okay?"

Angelo closed his eyes and breathed, his nostrils flaring. "Yeah, yeah. I'm... I'm okay."

"What's wrong? What happened?"

He sighed again, this time louder. "Nothing," he shook his head. "It's nothing."

"Hey, please, tell me." Alex' eyes were pleading.

Angelo looked at her worried face. "No, it's nothing, really. Let's clean up, and then we'll sleep, okay? Please don't worry about me. I'm okay. I'm okay."

Alex hugged him, "I hope you're telling the truth."

"I am." He wasn't. He just saw a statue - a statue that freaked him up with the first look – winked at him. It fricking winked! Figurines don't do that. There was something in that wink. It buries deep within his heart in the form of fear. A wink. A damn wink. Who in the blue hell loses his marbles by a wink?

She unfastened her arms around him, then kissed him in the cheek. "Come on, the dishes are not gonna wash themselves."

Chapter 5

After they finished, they stayed in the guestroom for a while, talking to pass the time. Before they had left for their little vacation, they had made each other swear not to use their phones unless absolutely necessary. None of them have broken that promise, so far. They were sitting on the bed beside each other, their backs leaning against the headboard.

"Is he always like that?" Alexandra asked suddenly when they were speaking of babies.

"No. That's why I was bothered with the way he acts. He's a good cook; our whole clan could testify to that. But he's also a modest person. He knows the different etiquettes. He wouldn't eat like a... pig in front of visitors."

"Well, he is close to you, so maybe he's just comfortable with our company."

"Even if he's alone, he wouldn't eat like that. *Pancit Canton* is like pasta. He would delicately twirl the fork and eat like he's an Italian food critic, like that guy from that animated movie."

"Well, people change. Maybe he's tired of acting so formal. Maybe he's comfortable with that manner. I mean, he lives alone. He can do whatever he wants."

"Have you seen him eat? He's like a baby!"

"You're a baby."

"Alex, I'm serious."

She held up her hand, stifling a giggle. "Okay, okay."

"I felt something: like I was being watched closely. Someone, or something felt... near."

Alex took one of the pillows and hugged it tight to her chest. "Me, too."

"I felt like there was something malignant nearby, watching us eat. I really can't explain it fully. It's the feeling that makes you paranoid. When I was a kid, we were watching one night a television show that featured a 'real life' horror story. You know, they always broadcast it every Halloween. Well, those stories scared the crap out of me. The make-up and the special effects were cheap, but the show didn't fail to scare me. I was literally trembling. The lights were turned off for the sake of establishing, you know, the atmosphere. Then someone poked me in the shoulder. I shouted and ran to my ma. Turns out, it was my brother."

"Anthony or Andrei?"

"Andrei. The buffoon was laughing while I was crying. 'Why do you overreact like that, you drama queen?' Mama told me."

"I think I know where you're going with this."

Angelo ignored her remark. "When we were having dinner, *that* feeling was building up inside me.

Every swallow of *Pancit* was a chore. Then I talked to uncle, you remember. Then I saw... I saw..."

"The saint."

"You knew?"

"I just had a feeling that it was it. I noticed the way you looked at that thing. I could see in your eyes that you wanted to smash it to pieces, but at the same time, dared not to."

"It winked at me."

Alexandra hugged the pillow tighter, then leaned closer to Angel.

"Then I overreacted. That—"

"Please," Alexandra interjected, making a gesture of dismissal with her hand. "Let's... let's not talk about this anymore. Maybe we're just tired. Remember, we have a big day tomorrow. I don't wanna ruin that with some... uh...."

Angelo smiled and chuckled. "Yeah, you're right. We'll have a great time tomorrow. We're not here to talk about all that garbage; we're here to have fun."

"Yes, so you better get some sleep because we have to wake up early."

"Yeah," he kissed Alex on her forehead. "Good night."

"Night."

Angelo went out of the room (bringing a couple of pillows and a blanket with him) and closed the door. He hadn't realized how dark the living room was without the lights on. He walked slowly, then once his vision adjusted to the darkness, he saw the faint silhouette of the long, wooden chair. He groped for it, and once he reached it, he started to lie down. He hugged one of the pillows and put the other under his head, and then he covered himself with the blanket.

Before he slept, he heard a faint, consecutive sound, like a marblehitting the floor.

Chapter 6

They had omelet and fried rice for breakfast. Gordon looked to be himself again. He was all smiles and giggles, but a reserved one. He was not eating like a pig, though the way he held the spoon was still pretty peculiar. His eyes seemed normal, jolly, even, unlike last night, when they had looked like the eyes of a paranoid drug addict.

And the damn figurine was absent. This was a relief to Alex and Angelo.

"You guys ready for later?" Gordon asked.

It was Alex who answered. "Yes. Our things are all packed."

"Excited?"

"Very," Angelo said, forcing himself to sound cheery. "We've been planning this for months. It's a great help that you let us stay with you. We are really grateful."

Gordon smiled and waved his hand. "No, no, it's nothing. I mean, I'm a part of the family, and that's what family do, right? We do favors to each other within our capacity. Besides, I can't say no to your Ma. She's like a sister to me; a sister and a best friend. And you, Angel, are like a son to me."

Angelo was deeply touched by this. Just last night, he called his uncle a pig and a baby. He suddenly felt bad.

"It's just too bad you have to leave so soon. You know, I've been lonely since your *Lolo* and *Lola* left and resided in Mindanao. Every time I have visitors, it feels like a *fiesta* here."

"Well," Angelo said while using his tongue to remove a grain of rice stuck between his teeth, "reunion's coming soon this Christmas. We will visit you here again."

Alex was smiling, genuinely happy for Tito Gordon; at the same time, she pitied him. According to Angel, Tito Gordon's fiancé had left him after she'd found out she had cancer. He was devastated.

"Reunions always cheer me up. I love how my nieces and nephews grow up. One day, they were small kids running around the yard, or crying or pestering their mother." He chuckled. "The next day they are high school or college students with girlfriends or boyfriends."

They heard a faint sound of the siren from an ambulance. They turned their heads in unison towards the open door.

"What happened?" Alex asked.

Gordon swallowed then said, "Freddy, the owner of the thrift store I told you about yesterday. He was found dead in his room. In his nightstand there was an open bottle of pills. People assumed that he had poisoned himself."

The two lost their appetite.

"Why?" Alex asked.

"No one really knows. As far as we know, he's financially stable. His family is in good state, though four years ago his youngest son died. But we were very convinced that he had moved on from that. So yeah, none of us could find a convincing motive."

"Maybe he's depressed," Angelo guessed. "Most victims of depression don't show that they are going through something. Sometimes, their loved ones would just find out once it's too late."

"God have mercy on his soul," Gordon muttered.

Angelo saw one corner of his uncle's mouth twitched.

Chapter 7

Death, or someone that's a victim of it, is not a pleasant topic during breakfast, they concluded.

After they washed the dishes, they rested for a bit before they prepared themselves. They decided to leave their phones since there was no signal at the beach, the brochure said.

They rode a jeepney and a tricycle before they reached the beach. There were a few people either sitting on the black sand or splashing salt water, but the place did not look isolated. They rented a cottage near the restrooms. They changed their clothes, took a shower, then ran towards the waves. They swam, splashed saltwater on each other, built a sandcastle that looked like a cow's turd.

Now they were sitting side-by-side in the sand. Alex's knees were up to her chest, and Angelo's were spread, relaxed. "It's nice to have each other here," he said. "You know, watching the waves and the sunset."

"I was hoping for a better view," Alex said. "But I guess it only happens in movies."

"But it doesn't matter."

"Correct."

Angelo took the stick lying beside him and drew a star on the sand, not sure why he did that.

"I can't wait for us to graduate," Alex said, "to grow old, to have a job of our own..."

Angelo folded his right leg. "And then we'll get married."

"And have children of our own. I hope our firstborn will be a boy."

"Yes."

"But we'll not name him Goku, or All Might,"

"Aww."

Alex chuckled.

"But we'll not name our daughter Hermione," Angelo countered. "Or Katniss, and especially not Dorothy Gale. I don't want her singing *Over the Rainbow* first thing in the morning."

"It's unfair," Alex pinched a few grains of sand with her fingers, then threw them at Angelo's face. "And that's a beautiful song."

He used his finger to remove the grains of sand that had gone inside his ear. "Regardless, I hope for us to be happy." He held her hand, not minding the people around them having their own time. "You know, I'm just glad that among seven billion people, you chose me to be yours."

"Aww, that's so sweet, but it's not really an accurate number. You have to subtract the number of females, married men, priests, boomers... I could go on, but I think you get my point. Get your logic straight next time before you try to flatter me."

"Oh... yeah. Haven't heard that before. I'm too lazy to do the math, so I'm not going to say that again."

They watched the people in the waves playing with each other. Each passing wave made them shout with glee.

"You think your Tito's okay?"

"I don't know. He was not himself last night, but he's quite okay this morning." Angelo drew several random lines over the star he had drawn, still oblivious to what he's doing. "I have to believe he's okay. Sometimes, I think, maybe we're just overthinking. The worst didn't happen yet. Maybe, there's nothing coming. Maybe we don't have to worry too much."

"Gosh, I keep forgetting our intention of going here. Let's not talk about that."

"I already told you that, but you still brought it up."

"I'm sorry."

"It's okay."

Angelo did not want to talk about it: his uncle's weird behavior, the winking figurine, none of it. He just wanted to flush it out of his mind, like a poop.

Chapter 8

It was already dark when they returned to Gordon's house.

They found Tito Gordon sitting on the floor in the living room, his back leaning against the wall. In his childish hands he held the figurine and had been twirling it with his fingers, right in front of his face. His eyes were wide, full of fascination, like a kid holding a chick for the first time. He smiled with his trembling lips, like he's on the verge of crying. "...Yes..." he muttered. "I've been a good boy, papa. I no bad boy. No dear." His voice was a bit squeaky. "Gordon's a good boy, papa. Yes, he is. A good—"

"Tito?" Angelo said.

Gordon shot up from his sitting position, holding the figurine to his chest, careful not to drop it or something. His childish smile was gone; his mouth was now an arch, forming several creases in the skin near the corners of his lips. His fascinated eyes were replaced by suspicious ones, as though the couple of brats standing in the doorway wanted to take his toy. "Hi," he said, grinning.

Angelo tilted his head slightly. "Are you okay?"

Then Gordon's expression was like a kid's who was caught drawing something inappropriate on the wall with a permanent marker. "Uh... I'm just... um... cleaning this... uh... I asked Freddy's assistant. He said this one," he held up the little saint with fake pride, "is a collector's item. He said these costs thousands, so I'm keeping it clean." He breathed at his new toy and wiped it with his t-shirt to make his point.

"Oh, okay." The couple went inside, not taking their eyes away from Gordon.

"You guys had fun?" Gordon said. He put the figurinein the pocket of his shorts, but the space wasn't enough, so that the imp of a saint appeared to be peeking while hiding.

Alex answered, "Yes, yes. We had."

Gordon nodded, "Nice. I'm gonna make dinner."

Alex nudged Angelo when Gordon headed to the kitchen, his back on them. Angelo faced her, mouthing *what?*

Her eyebrows joined in her forehead and she moved her eyes towards his uncle in the kitchen.

Angelo was not sure what that look meant, but he said. "Um... Tito. What can we do to help?"

They heard something banged: a pot dropped on the floor, causing a ringing sound that lingered in the air. And out of the kitchen, the uncle burst out, eyes wide (again, and this time with fury) and teeth baring like a dog. To Alex, the human Teddy bear was gone. He stopped a few feet from the two and pointed his finger at his nephew. "What are you trying to say, huh? That I can't cook by myself? That just like you said, I'm uncoordinated, like a baby? That I would need your help?" Gordon stepped closer to his nephew and held him by the collar of his shirt. "Is that what I am to you? A pig? A baby?"

"I didn't—"

"The hell you didn't! Papa told me!"

"Who—"

"He told me—" Gordon trailed off and looked at his hand holding his nephew's collar. The Teddy bear face slowly returned with the look of a little regret. Then he smiled brightly, his gums showcased. "How do you like hotdogs?"

"Huh?"

"Steamed or fried?" Gordon let go of the cloth.

Angelo's mouth gaped open. He couldn't answer so Alex did. "Fried." Gordon faced her abruptly; she could imagine a movie sound effect that would go well with it: the sound of a bone that snapped. It brought chills down Alex' spine. "Fried," she repeated, this time lower.

"Okay. I heard you. Fried hotdogs, coming right up!" He returned to the kitchen.

"What the hell?" Alex asked Angelo when Gordon was out of sight.

"I don't know," he said noncommittally, then went to the room. He lay in bed with a thump and bounced once.

Alex lay beside him and put her arm around him. He was trembling.

"There's something really odd with him," he whispered.

She didn't reply. Instead, she hugged him a bit tighter.

"Stupid crazy bastard."

"Shh."

"Fricking—"

"Gelo."

He sighed and sat and Alex followed suit, put her arm around him again and pulled him closer. He laid his head on her shoulder. "We'll leave. Tomorrow."

"What?"

"We'll leave tomorrow."

She leaned her head on his, "Okay. Whatever you want."

After a few minutes, they slept. Alex was snoring; Angelo was quiet.

Chapter 9

They were awakened by gentle knocks on the open door of the room. It was Gordon. "Lovebirds, dinner," he simply said before he disappeared.

They got up, washed their faces, and went to the dining table. Half a dozen hotdogs were on a white plate with a small pool of oil circling those. They thought the smell was heavenly. They sat quietly in their seats.

"I'm sorry. I couldn't cook anything else," Gordon said, not looking at them.

"It's okay," Alex said, "this smells good though. I really love these fried." She looked at Angelo. He was looking down at his plate, slouching. His hands were clasped together between his knees.

"Yeah, I love it, too. We used to chop them up first before we fry them. Come on. Dig in."

They did. They ate silently until Gordon talked.

"Angelo."

Angelo raised his head slowly to face his Tito.

"I'm sorry about earlier. I'm just going through something," he chuckled then put a spoonful of rice in his mouth. He looked down at his plate and chewed lazily.

"It's okay," Angelo said. "I understand."

"I just feel alone."

The couple looked at each other, then at Gordon.

"I mean... I was never married... and... I mean..."

It's a bit odd for the two to hear the man talk about his feelings during dinner, but they couldn't help but feel pity towards him. Angelo had never seen his uncle this low.

All the traces of childishness or fury were gone from his face. There was now only a pure humanity and fragility. They did not dare give a remark; they thought it would be better to remain silent and listen.

"My parents lived with me for a while," his eyes rolled up a bit, and his forefinger twitched for a few times, "about half a year." He smiled sweetly and bitterly at the same time. "That was the happiest six months of my life." His eyes were now wet. "But someone gave them the house at Mindanao, and they didn't even think twice; two days after the great news, they left me."

Alex started to feel something in her throat. She gulped, hoping it's not audible.

"You know, Angelo, how excited I am every time there's a reunion. I am always happy cooking for the family, and their compliments are more than enough compensation." He wiped his eyes. "But reunions don't last. After everyone leaves, I'll feel alone again. No laughs and giggles surrounding me. No one."

Now Alex's eyes were starting to get moist.

"I promised her, Valerie, my supposed-to-be wife, that it will be okay. We'll get married and still have children and we'll fight the damn cancer together. I said I'll never leave her side. I said I'll hold her hands. I said we'll grow old together longer. I promised her the world. I promised everything."

Alex held Angelo's hand under the table, the sweat from their palms mixing.

"But she's afraid. She forgot my love for her because she didn't believe it. Then, she left. I never heard from her again." He finally cried, putting his hands on his mouth and gasped convulsively. He closed his eyes and looked down, embarrassed to show his face. His snot was coming in and out of his nostrils.

Alex took the opportunity and wiped her eyes with the back of her hand. She put a spoonful of rice in her mouth and chewed. When she swallowed, the lump of rice seemed to be stuck in her throat.

"You can't imagine how thrilled I was when your mother asked me if you two could stay here. Even for a few nights, I will never feel the isolation," he smiled warmly at the both of them. "Thank you."

Still, the two didn't talk. They replied wtih sympathetic nods instead.

Gordon pressed his lips together, then spoke. "And I'm sorry for acting weird. I don't know, maybe it's caused by... you know, isolation."

Angelo nodded again and said, "We understand. We're humans." Then he offered him his smile.

Somewhere in the farthest corner of his mind, he heard the sound of marbles hitting the floor.

"I'll get water," Gordon said. He stood up and went to the kitchen.

Alex whispered at Angel. "So...?"

He sighed loudly. "I'm sorry. My mind's made up. We will leave tomorrow. I don't know how he would take it. I'll call Ma later to tell her we're leaving early."

Chapter 10

Gordon was already snoring in his room when Alex called Angelo to her room. He was making coffee for the two of them. There was a coffee maker at the top of the refrigerator, but he didn't know how to use it, so he just heated more than a couple of cups of water with the thermos.

"What?"Angelo asked when he entered the room.

Alexandra was holding their phones and showing it to Angelo. Her face was unreadable.

"Oh, god." All the days of saving money and working as a freelancer came back to him as he neared their phones. There were cracks like spider webs on the screen. They pushed the power button hoping for the screen to light up, but it didn't.

"What happened?"

"I don't know," Alex replied. "We didn't bring them to the beach, right?"

"Look at the crack. It has an impact point. It looks like it's been hit with a hammer or something." They traced the cracks with their fingers from the center to the snaking lines that ended at the edge of the screen. A few crystal grains stick to the tips of their fingers. "Your important files are there, you said, for your thesis."

Alex scratched her cheek, "yeah... but they're safe in my Google Drive. What about your files? Henry said you got some videos there on your secret file fold—"

Angelo gave her a look of slight irritation.

She sighed. "What do you think happened?"

"It's him," Angelo said without a trace of hesitation. "I just know it's him." He kept his voice low, even though their room had a good distance from the snoring man's room. "You'd be crazy to doubt it."

"How could you say that?"

"Who else would do it? It's unlikely an accident. We didn't use our bags as pillows. We didn't sit on them. We didn't take them out and smash them with a rock. We've barely touched them since we came here."

"Hey," Alex touched Angelo's arm. "Just because there's something going on with him, it doesn't mean he'll go as far as this," she pointed to their phones. "It's *cum hoc ergo propter hoc*. Or is it *post hoc er*—"

"I don't know what the hell you're talking about. I just have this feeling that he did this. And don't tell me none of your mind's dimension doesn't believe that this didn't happen by accident."

Alex didn't answer.

"Sleep. We'll leave early."

"But you haven't told him."

"I'm not planning to. I have a feeling—"

Alex sighed with exasperation. "That feeling again."

Angelo held her shoulders and faced her, their face almost touching. "Tell me you don't feel something off. Tell it to my face. Tell me all I'm feeling is pure bullcrap. Tell me I'm just going crazy, too. Come on."

Alex stared at his eyes, seeing no fury in them. Only some sort of... desperation.

"Sleep," he said. "We're leaving early. We won't wait for the sun to come out."

When Angelo was halfway to the door, Alex said, "I don't think you're losing your mind. I will never think of you that way, because I love you."

He nodded while smiling. He turned away from her and went outside the room. *I love my uncle, too, because he's family,* he thought as he navigated through the dark living room.

What he had meant to say to Alex was, "I have a feeling that if we tell him we're leaving, he will not let us."

Chapter 11

He dreamt. He was wearing a black suit with a bowtie. On his left chest, there's a flower pinned; he couldn't recognize what type.

Beside him was an old man wearing a green robe and was smoking three sticks of cigarettes in his mouth, simultaneously clicking his tongue. The sound reminded Angelo of something, but he couldn't remember, and couldn't care less. All he knew was this man was a priest, and this man's going to officiate a wedding.

He couldn't recognize the place, but it was empty except for the incoming two people.

In the aisle, Alex was walking. Instead of a veil, she was wearing a cap that also looked familiar. But her white dress was beautiful. Phenomenal. Her hand was in the arms of the man beside her. It was Rando, his favorite barber.

The next moment, Angelo and Alexa ndra were face to face, holding each other's hand. The priest in the green robe said a few words that he couldn't understand until the priest clearly uttered the phrase "You may now kiss the bride."

As their lips touched, ecstasy came over him, among other things: extreme contentment, excitement, and confusion.

Chapter 12

He woke up, his lips still protruding, and his heart was pounding.

He looked outside through the window. It was still dark, so there's a good chance that midnight had just passed. How the hell would he know? His phone was smashed.

He walked blindly through the dark living room, then returned to the long wooden wood and lay there. He closed his eyes and tried to sleep to return to his wonderful dream; to put the ring on her finger, and to let her put the ring on his finger. He smiled at the thought. He urged himself to doze off.

But his eyes were not heavy anymore. He lay while his eyes closed for more than ten minutes before his eyelids got tired of being closed. He sat up, not sleepy anymore. Wakefulness punched him in the face. Maybe the hardness of the wooden chair kept him from returning to his wedding.

Maybe...

Maybe I could sleep beside her. She won't know I slept on the bed until she wakes up... if she wakes up first. Gosh, I wanna sleep in that soft mattress so bad. I'd return to my wedding once my back got a taste of that softness.

He walked slowly towards the room, careful not to make a noise at every step. His fingers found the surface of the door, and in no time found the doorknob. Then, before he turned it, he just noticed the faint light that spilled under the room's door. It's definitely not the light from a bulb, but from a candle. *What the hell is she doing?*

He opened the door and a strange coldness rushed in his face. He went inside...

Then he saw her.

He saw Alex.

His knees hit the floor; his mouth was wide open, and so were his eyes. He trembled.

There was Alex, the girl he first met at the canteen of their school, eating alone. She had had braces and was wearing glasses. He had walked towards her and handed her the paper. "Hello," he had said, "can I interview you?" She looked up at him with those eyes. *God, those eyes... those eyes are cosmic.* "It's for um... our assignment. If you have time." She smiled and took the paper. He hadn't realized it's improper to interview someone eating. He watched as her fingers held his pen. *This beautiful girl touched my pen oh my god!* When she had finished, she returned him the filled-out form, and smiled, those braces glinting in the sunlight. "Thank you," he said.

"I'll ask you to answer mine later," she had said to him. *Oh her voice was heavenly.* "We have the same assignment."

He had nodded, aggressively, he worried. "Sure, sure. He had left the canteen, holding the form delicately. He wore his smile for a long time.

It had not been love by then, but it's not too long before it became one.

Then that beautiful, lovely girl was now hanging, naked except for her underwear. The bamboo bed was standing (still parallel to the door), its four feet now touching the wall. Alex was there. Her arms were raised, forming a Y. Above her was the headboard. Her hands and wrists were nailed to the upper part bamboo bed. From the wounds of her hands and wrists, two thin streams of blood ran down to her smooth arms, to her armpits, to either side of her body. The blood soaked her white underwear, turning its sides red. Then the streams continued to flow down her legs. The blood dripped from the tip of the toes of her feet (which were just a few inches above the floor), making a small puddle of blood under her. There were also streams of blood running down the bed onto the floor.

Drool started to fall from Angelo's mouth. The shock was being thrust into his heart, slowly, like a rusty nail.

Alexandra's chin was touching her chest; her hair was hanging over her head, obscuring it. Angelo thought that if he peeked through her curtain of hair, he would see her eyes half-opened, and/or her mouth in a permanent grimace. He looked at her arms and shoulders; they were not rising and falling. She was still as a statue, as a figurine.

"Alexandra..." he whispered. That was when he sobbed. Then he shouted... no, he shrieked. It seemed that the small fire of candles on the floor that surrounded the nailed girl reacted; they jerked back as if horrified by the sound of the cry.

He stood up, wanting to step inside that half-circle of candles and hug her and feel her warmth on his cheek; he wanted to know that she's alive. He could call an ambulance (using someone else's phone). He could caress her hair while the doctors carefully remove the nails that impaled her hands and wrists, and he would sing for her. He would kiss her forehead repeatedly.

But even before he made a step, he felt something in his neck, and then he knew that it was a rope, a rough one, closing his windpipe. The momentum made him hit the floor, but the rope remained choking him.

"You know," the voice said in his ear. He could feel and smell his breath, "when you tilt her head upwards, you'll see a ring of black and red and purple around her neck, like a dog's collar."

The rope held tighter. He clawed at his neck; his feet kicked wildly, bringing down a couple of candles in the process. His eyes bulged from their sockets.

His vision was filled by the face of a man with a fake brown beard and mustache. His eyes were jovial, his cheeks were rosy, and his teeth were crooked. "Wanna take a look?" Then he laughed maniacally.

Gordon started to drag him outside the room. When his torso was outside, he hooked his leg to the wall. Then he made his other leg move. This was a struggle with suffocation overtaking him slowly.

Finally, he managed to stand up. The rope left his sore neck, and he gasped and coughed. Before his blurry vision focused, Gordon pushed him hard. He flew back into the room and fell on a few candles. The small fires kissed his back before they were extinguished.

He stood up and saw Gordon as a whole: He was wearing a green robe, and on its chest was an inverted star drawn with something red. He was wearing a wig and a fake mustache and beard. He was the human version of the figurine.

"What did you do?" Angelo asked his uncle with a trembling voice. "What have you done?"

Gordon spread out his arms and wore his wide grin again. "How'd you like it, *pamangkin?*"

"You lunatic! You killed her!"

"I have no choice! Papa asked me to! He said the candles were not required, but I thought it'd be cool if–" then without finishing his sentence, he brought out something from under his robe: it was a nail gun. "You like my new toy?"

Angelo glanced at Alex's hand and wrist. He thought big nails were impaling her, but he knew if he takes a closer look, he would see many small nails forming a bigger circle.

"It was kind of expensive, but papa told me he'll give me everything once I'm done with you, too. He was locked up for a long time, so I can only imagine how hungry he is right now."

"You're out of your mind."

"We're all out of our minds!" Then he charged at Angelo, the nail gun on his other hand.

In a matter of seconds, every memory he had had with his uncle dissolved. The man charging at him was not the man who had attended his graduation in 6th grade, or the one who had brought him to a mall and bought him a Power Rangers toy when his father was sent to the hospital due to the accident. He was not his mother's and father's best friend. Those memories weren't hard to flush out; looking at the love of his life that had been nailed to a bed for god knows how long made it much easier.

He let the man come at him. The impact brought them down hard, and Angelo's head almost hit the wall on the bed's right; he was under the man. He felt the man's hands grab his neck tightly. Once again, Angelo was suffocating.

"I strangled her to death before I took off her clothes and nailed her. Papa wants me to do the same to you, but I guess you're stubborn and strong unlike her. Look at my cheek. See that red line? She did that. That's the only thing she had managed to do."

Angelo was holding tight to his uncle's shoulder and tried to push him away, but with his situation, it was just impossible.

"I think I just have to end things quickly with you. Say hello to your father for me, would you?" Gordon put the nail gun's nose to Angelo's forehead.

Panic boiled inside Angelo. His heart beat a hundred times faster. Using his knee, he hit the lunatic in the butt with a force he'd never released before. The lunatic went forward and bumped his head on the wall. He unrolled from his nephew and just lay beside him in a fetal position, holding his head with two hands.

Angelo saw the nail gun just within his reach (and out of the man's hand) and took it. He stood up, having vertigo. Meanwhile, the madman was muttering curses.

Angelo brought the nail gun to the man's left knee and pulled the trigger. The man's whole body jerked as he shouted. His hands left his head and found his nailed knee. "You bastard!"

"You're not yourself anymore," Angelo's moral principles and fear of the consequences of a murder disintegrated as fast as the vanishing of his good memories with his uncle. "You are someone else." He shot the madman's another knee and another cry rang out again, but this time a bit restrained. Angelo figured that this nail gun was a more ideal weapon because it's quieter and less damaging, making the agony much longer, which was the exact thing he wanted to inflict right now. Angelo shot the maniac again, this time without pausing, at his feet, shoulders, elbows, belly, groin, teeth, chin, and eyes. Each shot came with a shrill and a curse and a slight splatter of blood.

Angelo looked at his creation. The man wasn't holding a single hole in his body; he'd need forty-six hands if he wanted to do that.

"I shouldn't have come here," he said with a voice full of regret.

The man moaned and was shivering.

Apparently, there's a little mercy left in him. He shot the man in the head ten times; twice in each temple, and six times in the forehead. The man made a series of spasms then went still.

Chapter 13

Angelo went out of the room and went to the kitchen. He turned on the lights. On the rim of the sink, there's a sealed envelope. He tore off the top of it and brought out the folded paper and opened it. It was from Freddy, the owner of the thrift store. In the paper it said:

I shouldn't have given it to you.

That's all. He then crumpled the paper and threw it in the trash bin.

He wanted to go to the room and bring down Alex and hold her. He wanted to cradle her in his arms or to just sit while her head's on his lap, but he didn't have the guts to come near her. He was afraid. He didn't see her face. What if the woman nailed to the bed wasn't Alex? No, it was her. He knew her.

He went to the living room and turned on the light. He looked through the window and it was still dark. He sat on the chair he'd been sleeping on. He wanted to cry. He wanted to cry himself to sleep. He wanted to cry himself to death.

Something caught his attention.

Right there in the middle of the dining table was the figurine. It was broken into several pieces.

He returned to the chair and lay. Soon, someone would find out what had happened, and he'd be the one to blame, of course. Who else was alive in the house?

But for now, he just wanted to sleep, to dream again of the wedding, hoping that dream was the reality, not this nightmare he was in.

He dreamt of the man in the green robe instead.

End

Diary

Chapter 1

There were several fans holding their phones and taking videos of the event.

On stage was Linda Baltazar, author of four novels published internationally. In front of her were several of her readers, mostly students, seated, listening to her speak about books, writing, and her life.

"At a young age, I knew I'm going to be a writer," she said. In her hand was a microphone; on the other was a bottle of water. "I would write anything, anywhere. Whenever I was bullied, I would sit in the corner of the classroom, take my notebook, and write a short story about me killing the sons of bitches." The audience laughed. She saw her husband, who was among the listeners, laugh, too. "It's a bit of fun, writing, I mean. It's the only way I can kill legally."

She spent another half an hour talking. She told the story of how she found Jesse, her husband, at a rally; she entertained her audience with her stories of her editor, Markus, whom she often made fun of. Her editor is cool with that. In her second book, on the acknowledgement page, she thanked her editor for helping her make the book better and for assuring her that she would never be the ugliest person in the world because there would always be Markus.

After that is the Q&A of the event. A thin man with a cap asked, "you mentioned that there was an author you met, and one of his books inspired your first novel, *The Unknown Friend*. Who is this author?"

Linda cleared her throat. "Um... it's not my habit to mention the names of my inspirations when it comes to my books and other fictional works. I want the readers to figure out for themselves who's that inspiration. But I'll give you a clue. He was very famous. One work of his was actually translated into Spanish. He promised his fans a novel about a psychopathic serial killer, I think, but there was no follow-up after that. Then, he just completely stopped writing for some reason."

The man with the cap thanked her, nodded, and sat down.

Other questions followed. About her writing habits, her love for literature; her next book that will be published by Christmas or New Year, and other typical queries. She had fun answering these questions. There was one question that made her utter a spoiler. As soon as she realized, she covered her mouth and said "oh crud."

"Mrs. Baltazar will only answer one last question," the emcee said, who was sitting among the audience and holding a microphone to her mouth.

Seven raised their hands. Linda chose a woman with glasses who was holding a paperback copy of her third book.

"I'm a huge fan of your works," the woman with the glasses said, smiling widely, her face red, like she was on the verge of exploding. "I read everything you wrote that was published in newspapers and magazines."

"Thank you, dear," Linda said.

"My favorite novel of yours is this one." The woman held up the book she was holding. It had a simplistic cover design; the size of the letters wasn't shouting; the illustration of a grinning old lady wasn't intricate. "The characters in this story are so real. I just want to ask, what is the origin of this book?"

Linda gulped, quite audibly, since she was using a mic. "That... *The neighbors*. I'm glad you liked it. Well..." she studied the audience. Their eyes were glued to her, expecting her answer. She looked around, as if asking for help. She met the gaze of Jesse, who raised his eyebrows and mouthed *what*. "You see—"was she stammering? She desperately hoped she was not. "Um... it's just the movies I've watched." She shrugged. "I just patched the ideas together and created that." She gestured her hand towards the questioner's copy of *The Neighbors*.

The questioner smiled awkwardly and said her thanks. She sat down, although her face showed dissatisfaction with Linda's answer.

Linda rested her elbow on the podium and breathed deeply. "I think that's it." She smiled at her listeners and thanked them for coming. Again, she promoted her upcoming book. The audience responded with applause. She saw her husband give her a two thumbs-up.

The emcee went to the stage, shook Linda's hand, thanked her, and handed her a framed certificate. "Our school is looking forward to having you again."

Linda smiled, quite forcefully, and said, "Yes, yes. We'll see. I love meeting you all."

That was the last time she publicly spoke as an author.

Chapter 2

The certification was followed by a book-signing. She autographed hundreds of books. Her fingers were sore.

She and her husband had returned home after that tiring day. She was on their bed; the blanket was up to her waist. Jesse entered their room.

"They're asleep?" Linda asked.

"Yes."

Their two daughters were Linda's splitting image. They inherited Jesse's height. The younger, Agatha, showed an early interest in writing, while Christie, the oldest, showed a passion for visual arts. One of Christie's drawings of her parents was taped to the wall of the couple's room. There were words under that drawing; it was Agatha's poem:

> *Mommy and Daddy*
> *love each other dearly*
> *they hold hands and kiss*
> *don't do it in front of us please*

Jesse lay beside Linda. "That's a good one you did right there," he said and kissed Linda on the cheek.

"Thank you," Linda said. "I'm afraid I was stammering badly."

"You didn't. Well, you actually did, but only once. When you mentioned the name of the author of The Little Prince."

"Yeah. That." She laughed. She looked her husband straight in the eyes. "Let's celebrate this fine day."

Jesse grinned. "How?"

"You know how I want it," she said, then kissed him on the lips, her hands combing the hair on the back of his head.

They undressed each other and made love. It was as sweet as the first time they did it.

They lay beside each other after they finished, panting. Linda's head was resting on Jesse's shoulder. "I love you."

"I know."

There was silence, not an awkward one, until Jesse said. "Linda."

"What."

"Remember that question that was asked to you?"

"There were over ten questions. Which one?"

"The last one."

"Oh. That."

"Yes."

"So, what's with that?" Jesse's hand was on her chest. She hoped he didn't feel her heart hammering.

"I noticed something with you. You sounded like you were hesitant to answer her question."

"So?"

"It's just a simple question."

"Yes."

"So why did it look like you're answering a hard one?"

"I just don't want to answer it, that's all."

"But you answered it. You said it was a patch-up work of several movies you've watched."

"Yes."

"I haven't read any of your books."

"Yeah. So ungrateful."

Jesse stifled a laugh. "Okay, I'll read one. Where do you want me to start?"

Linda sat up. "The first one, of course. *The Unknown Friend*."

"Is it good?"

"It has a pretty high ratings, so..."

"I want to start with the third one. What's it called? Yeah. *The Neighbors*."

Linda reached for her shirt and wore it. "Why would you wanna read it?"

"It just seems interesting."

"Suit yourself."

Jesse got up from the bed and walked to the corner of their room. There was a bookshelf with paperbacks stacked in it. On the first layer were multiple copies of Linda's books: *The Unknown Friend, The Tombstone in My Room, The Neighbors,* and her latest book, *Coffin Yards*. Jesse took a copy of the third book and returned to bed. He leafed through the pages.

"So?" Linda said.

"This is too long. Might take me a month."

"An average reader would finish it in three days. Four days tops."

"Oh, well, I'm slow. Sorry for that." Jesse closed the book and reached for his wife and kissed her. "I'm so proud of you. You're still not in your thirties, but you've already published four books."

"Don't be surprised," Linda said. "Many authors younger than me have published more. It's just a matter of dedication... and luck, I guess."

"Yeah. Right." Jesse read the synopsis on the back cover of the book. "'Perez family just moved in on a subdivision. The place looks nice; it is affordable, and the neighbors are friendly, too friendly.' Oh. Something is definitely wrong with the neighbors." He turned to his wife for confirmation.

Linda only shrugged. "I don't know, maybe."

"Well, I won't read the synopsis. The story might be spoiled."

"Who the hell puts a spoiler in the synopsis?" Linda said, amused.

"I dunno." Jesse turned the book on the first page.

Linda let him read, watching his eyes move and his mouth mutter silently. She watched him as he licked his thumb and turned the page. "Wait," she interrupted.

Jesse turned to her. "What?"

"I... I need to tell you something about that book."

"What?"

"It's not inspired by the movies I've watched. That's rubbish."

"Um... okay."

"It was based on... real events. Real story. I haven't told anyone but you."

He stared at her, dumbfounded. Then he looked at the book he was holding. There was something with the subtle way the wrinkles on his face deepened; he looked afraid he might be electrocuted by the paperback he was holding anytime. "Really?"

"Yes."

"Care to tell me the... uh... origins? Whose story is this?"

"Wilbert."

"Who's that? Is he a friend of yours?"

"No. I don't personally know him, and he doesn't know me."

"Huh?"

"Wait." She stood up and walked to a drawer; it was not far from the bookshelf. She pulled the lowest slide. Inside it was a box. She took it out and opened it.

"What is it?" Jesse asked. He was ignored.

Inside the box were old albums, documents, thesis, and other papers Linda has no recollection of writing. She rummaged and finally took a red notebook. Its cover was designed with several creases. The pages were wilted and had water stains, but were still intact. Around a quarter of the pages of the notebook, a bookmark was jutting. She set the notebook aside, closed the box, and returned it inside the drawer. She returned to bed with the notebook in her hand.

"What's that?"

"You asked for origins, right? We still weren't married when I found this," Linda said.

"What's that?" asked her husband again.

"The origin of *The Neighbors*. Remember that Christmas when you and your family went to Hong Kong?"

"Yes. It was also a late celebration of my brother's graduation."

"Yes. While you were away, one day, Kat, you know her, right? She celebrated her twentieth birthday at her home in Makati. She invited me and Mags and JR, Mags' boyfriend. We rode a bus to go there. On the way home, I rode alone. The couple stayed for a week more. I had to go home because my Lola would be visiting from Visayas."

"May she rest in peace."

"Yeah, yeah. So where was I? Yup, I was riding the bus. I sat in the last row. You know, the long seat. That is my favorite spot. I always prefer sitting there. So anyway, I found this—" she held up the notebook— "on the seat. I sat and ignored it at first. Then, I got bored and took a peek. When I figured out it was a diary, I immediately closed it, because I didn't want to invade someone's privacy."

Jesse took the notebook from her and examined it.

"I decided to bring that home and call the owner. When I got home, I examined the contents, not necessarily enthusiastically reading the entries. I was just looking for a name, but there were only first names. No surnames. I don't know who is Wilbert, or who is Jericho."

"Have you tried posting it online?" Jesse asked.

"That did not cross my mind. Besides, I did not have a phone at the time."

"Why haven't I heard of this earlier?"

Linda stared at the blank wall. "Because... I feel like I shouldn't tell anyone."

"You're not making any sense."

"I..." she sighed deeply. "Look at the last page."

Jesse did just that. Words were written:

BURN THIS PLEASE

"It said just burn it," Jesse said. "The owner wants to get rid of it. Why did you read it?"

"Curiosity. The message got me curious. I read the last entry. It doesn't make sense. It ended just like that, like a cliff-hanger. I read all the entries to understand the context." Her voice began to shake. "I was hoping to help, maybe investigate or something. I planned to ask the authorities' assistance. That might be an important piece of evidence or something."

Jesse looked at her, lost.

"Just read it. Things might make more sense to you."

Jesse gave the notebook to his wife. There was a slight disgust in his face. "I'm not just gonna read someone's life. That's absurd. And if you thought it was of importance or something, why didn't you give it to the authorities? You made a novel out of it instead."

"There may be a reason why Wilbert wanted it to be burned. And I had a dream."

"What dream?"

"Just a dream."

"I won't read that diary of Wilbert, whoever the hell he is."

"Then don't," Linda said sternly.

Jesse exasperated. "Ah, shoot. Fine! I still don't know what the hell went on with that diary. Once I've finished, you have more explaining to do."

Chapter 3

March 21, 2015, Sn

Liar liar burn on fire. She asked me to wait because she's not ready. She only wants to be my friend. But when the right time comes, she'd give me a chance. She said this about a week ago.

Then I saw she was with a man. Gosh, he's tall and he has good hair. The complete opposite of me. Her arm was on his. They were chatting happily.

It's unfair that she asked me to wait, but she won't wait herself.

Good night. Gonna cry myself to sleep.

yawn.

March 22, 2015, M

We played basketball in the court. Whole court. We lost badly. Jericho was such a wimp. I wanted to drag him across the whole subdivision. Of course I'd make sure that his face would be scraped until there's no skin left.

He bought me a coke and a bag of potato chips. I forgave him.

But I will not forgive that liar of a woman. May her guy poop his pants at school.

I mean, what didn't she like about me? Is it because I'm a minor and she's like, 19? I'm gonna be 18 in August! Why couldn't she wait?

Nah. It's more logical to think that she didn't like me. Because I'm ugly and I'm.... no, I'm not ugly. The guy is ugly. God, what a poor taste she has.

I'm not gonna cry myself to sleep like last night. Mama was worried.

March 23, 2015

I made a funny joke when we had breakfast. lol!

We had fried tilapia with fried rice. Papa cooked the rice. It was good. Kuya Wally cooked the fish. He burned them. Haha what an idiot.

Mama asked me if I'm doing well in class. I said not quite. But I also said I'm gonna do well next time.

That's a joke. Laugh goshdarn you.

Yep. So after that, I went to school. My math teacher surprised us with a quiz. We protested that he didnt announce anything. He said that we should always review our lessons to be prepared. He's such a doosh.

What else to tell...

Nothing much happened. My classmates are as boring as always. Some of them seriously need to start taking thorough baths. But still tolerable, nottheless.

Well, another boring day of Wilbert. Good night!

March 24, 2015, T

I spilled my coffee all over my uniform when I was having breakfast. I cursed. Mama slapped my mouth. Kuya laughed. Mama twisted his ears.

School. School. Nothing new. Wait, there was. I know we're high school students. Grown ups. We're nearing college, but there is still the tendency to act like babies. Our class president and Ivan fought. What fun! We literally cheered. Fight! Fight! Fight! Fight! The two ended up getting suspended. Lol!

So, yup. That's today high lights. Good night.

I still hate her.

March 25, 2015, W

Report. I wasn't prepared. Good thing, my groupmate Ireen was. Bad thing, her visual aids are trash.

Yep. We both got low grades. She blamed me, of course. I didn't blame her. From time to time I still laugh at the way she had mispelled a word. She wrote asspiring instead of aspiring. Get it? Ass-piring? Ha ha ha!

I went home and played basketball. Again, Jericho was a crap player. Again I forgave him. He mentioned about the multiple new families settling in our subdivision. New neighbors. Yey. I hope to meet some new girl. Not a liar one.

Good night! To you. I'm not sleeping yet. I'm going out with Jericho and Gabriel. We're gonna drink beer all night. My father does not know (as far as I know). Mama is also oblivius.

We're gonna get messed-up and we're gonna paint the subdivision red! Woo hoo!.

March 26, 2015, Th

time check: 2:13. Damn. Kind of wasted. I don't know if I'm gonna be able to make it to school.

update: I was able to. But just imagine what I look like while listening to teachers.

So, some news:

Am I sad that I'm gonna be left out? Depends. Are they going to the beach? Or a theme park? Then I'm gonna feel down. Are they visiting my dying auntie and staying there until she is buried? Of course, not. I hate funerals. I hate burials.

I only met Tita twice in my life, and we only talked once, when she asked me to buy a case of beers for my pot-bellied uncles. We're not really close, but she and kuya are.

They said tita is dying. They said it's a brain tumor. She thought it was just a migraine. They still don't have an estimated duration of their stay there, but they said it's gonna be more than a week.

I'm gonna be alone in the house for a week? Am i in heaven? Lol.

So yeah. They're gonna leave by monday. Yay.

Here are some pre-reminders from mama:

1. Always make sure the door is locked every time I go out.

2. Don't forget to turn off the gas after cooking

3. Clean, of course

I am thinking of something else, but I think that's it.

Night!

March 27, 2015, F

Friday. I love friday.

I got perfect scores in our Filipino quiz. I was so proud of myself before I knew that almost everyone got perfect score. That's no fun. I might sound a bit of a nincompoop here by saying this, but I don't want anyone to have the same victory I have. Yeah. Hell to those classmates of mine. May you get zero in the next quiz.

Am I worried about being a jackass here? Of course not. Who else would read my diary 'cept me?

After school, I didn't play basketball. There was no slot for another player. Jerks.

So I just watched TV.

My parents went to the market and bought some supplies for me. They said they'll give me extra money just in case the supplies wouldn't be enough. If the money wouldn't be enough, then I'll just borrow some from a neighbor.

'Sall. Good night!

update: They were happy together. Fools.

March 28, 2015, St

I saw a bald guy walking in our streets this morning. He was checking the houses that are to be occupied by new families/new neighbors. Everything is set, I heard a man in uniform said. Suppose he's the one taking care of things. I dunno. I don't know how the system works.

Regardless, I'm kinda excited. I really do hope there'll be a girl. A beautiful one. Hehe. Please.

We had fried chicken for dinner. I cooked. Kind of raw. Papa was pissed off.

Nothing much happened this afternoon.

Good night.

March 29, 2015, Sn

Mama and Papa went to church. Kuya went out with his friends. I was left alone.

I saw the trucks. Men carried things. Furniture, TV, and other house things. There are only two families. Two houses are occupied.

Yay. New neighbors.

Here are the members of the two families from what I saw:

First house:

- *A man. Prolly the same age as papa.*
- *A woman. Same age as mama*

- *An old lady. Old but looks strong*
- *A girl. Probably 10.*
- *A boy. An exact copy of the girl. Probably her twin*
- *A boy. Maybe fifteen. Or sixteen. Younger than me, probably, but not too young. I don't know.*

Second House:

- *The bald man yesterday*
- *A woman. A bit older than Mama.*
- *A man in his twenties, maybe.*
- *And a girl, about my age. YES!*

She's beautiful. In fact, I made a haiku for her:

Your eyes are so deep

your smile is so rich, really

I'm in love, believe me.

Shit. A syllable longer. Nah. Who cares.

Anyway, she smiled at me. I saw beautiful girls smiling at awkward guys at movies, especially RomComs, but I did not imagine it happening in real life. but it happened. I almost melted. Yeah yeah I know it's not a thing. What am I, The Wicked Witch of the West? And no, I did not watch the movie, but I read the book. The only book I read this year.

Lol.. That's it. Looking forward to meeting my new neighbors. Night!

March 30, 2015, M

The storage is full of supplies. I already compartmentalized them. Everything is distributed evenly. Mama gave me an extra two thousand pesos. She told me not to spend it unless absolutely necessary.

They left around 5 o'clock.

I went to school and was welcomed with great news. School year is ending. And it sank in. I'm gonna be college next school year. Ah, gosh.

Anyway, the signing of clearance has started. I would probably finish it by tomorrow.

Then pictorial.

Then preparation of graduation.

Then, graduation!

Thrilled.

Well, not as thrilled as meeting my new beautiful neighbor.

The newly-occupied houses face each other. From time to time the new occupants come out, sweeping the front of their houses, just taking a view of the street, all that stuff.

I was coming back from school when the father of the first home, I presume, saw me and greeted me.

He said How am I. I said I'm good. He asked me where could he buy supplies like scotch tape, pens, etc. I told him about Aling Fatima's store. I told him it is near the court. You'll see a red car with Hellboy design. He thanked me and went on.

I saw Jericho. He was carrying a couple of tray of Lumpia. He said it was a greeting to our new neighbors. His mother made them. I took one of the trays and told him I'd give the tray to the second home, the one with a parked Van in front. My chance to meet my future love of my life.

I did not tell Jericho that we have new pretty neighbor. I have no intention of telling him.

So I knocked on the door and guessed who opened it? My new crush. I stammered. I don't know what I said. I was lost. I think I said the tray of lumpia was from a neighbor (I nodded towards Jericho whose, back was on us. whew). I said it's a greeting. And her smile. Oh god, her smile. Her teeth are perfect. Her eyes were a bit bigger but in a beautiful way.

Unfortunately, the girl shouted her thanks to Jericho. Jericho waved and smiled and proceeded to face the Lola of the first house. They're talking, and Jericho seemed eager. Wow.

So yeah. She thanked me too and closed the door. She said her name's Mia. Wow. Mia. I love you Mia.

Her voice is so... well, a bit manly, but in a beautiful way.

Damn. I'm smiling right now while writing this. Hoping to talk to her again.

Oh wow (Owen Wilson's version. Whoew.), this one's a long entry. Probably the longest.

What can I say? Love can make you do crazy things.

Good night.

March 31, 2015, T

I did all the things I needed to do at school. Just a few matters to consider, then I'm up to the stage.

On the way home, I saw the mother of the second house. She was hanging wet clothes on a cord. She saw me and greeted me. I greeted back. She looks nothing like her daughter. If it's her daughter. I haven't asked.

So I went inside my home and slept. It wasn't that thrilling being alone.

When I woke up, I went to the court. We only played half-court.

Then I saw the girl of my dreams walking. She was with the twin from the first home. They were holding ice cream cones. The fifteen-year-old boy was also with them. They are her cousins. She told me later.

The players's head turned to the or new neighbors. But none of them uttered a single word. My teammate passed the ball to me. I made sure Mia was looking at me before I shoot.

I missed. By a long shot.

The sun was already set when I went home. I saw her with her cousins. I did not approach her because I'm embarrassed of course. But she waved at me and introduced her cousins to me. I said my high. The twin girl smiled at me. The other two boys remained silent.

I went to the kitchen and began cooking egg. I was smiling so wide. Crap. She talked to me.

Right now, I'm smiling again.

Huh. Weird. Something hit the window of my room. Sounds like a knock. I opened it and there was nothing. Might be a bird or a bat.

So yep. That's it. Night!

April 1, 2015, W

I didn't go to school. My teacher said we don't have to until the start of graduation ceremony practice.

When I went out, the two cars of the two new homes were gone. I guess they left to go to the mall or something.

Nothing happened much. I just played basketball again and we won. After that, just the usual routine. The sky darkened and my new neighbors haven't arrived yet.

Good night.

Wait. I heard their cars. I opend my door a bit and saw them getting out, carrying boxes. New home furniture, I guess. Going out to help them crossed my mind, but I'm embarrassed.

April 2, 2015, Th

This is one of my happiest days. Mia saw me taking out the trash. She approached me with her smile. Her cosmic, magical, beautiful, awesome, terrific, amazing, supercalifragilisticexpialidocious smile. At first, I stuttered again. She laughed like a conservative maiden. Grah!

We just exchanged infos about our family. The two families are relatives. The old woman at the first home is her grandmother. I gave my own family info. My mother, father, and stinky older brother.

We talked some more about our school, all that stuff. There were silences in between. Pretty awkward.

Before she left, she patted my shoulder and smiled more. oh gosh.

Sheesh. Getting sleepy. Good night!

April 3, 2015, F

Time check. 2:15am. I heard footsteps outside. Pacing back and forth. I went out and saw no one. On the pavement were several burned out matchsticks. Those fricking kids, I thought. Manong Geraldo's notorious sons. They were always a pain in the ass for littering.

I woke up, around 10am. I cooked my breakfast, and went out. I went to Jericho's house and asked for him. His father said he went out with his mother. They went to the hospital.

The cars of my new neighbors were once again gone. I was assuming so was my new neighbor.

But around... two in the afternoon? Prolly three, Mia knocked on my door. She asked me to help her with the assembly of their electric fan. Am I a fool to say no?

So yup. Something weird happened. God, I would bury myself if any of my family read this.

So, I went inside and saw the electric fans. They were all assembled. She locked the door. I asked her what needs fixing.

She said none. She asked me if I have a girlfriend. I said none. She said she does not have a boyfriend. I told her I'm not getting her. Then not very gently she pushed me onto the sofa. I sat. She sat beside me. She smiled at me. Then she kissed me squarely in the lips, her hand on my thigh. It lasted for three seconds before I broke the paralysis and stood up and went out.

I slammed the door of my house shut. My hormones should be going crazy that time, but no. I felt... dirty. Until now.

Gosh. It's making me uncomfortable.

bye. Night.

April 4, 2015, St

I had my confrontation.

Someone knocked and thankfully it wasn't Mia. It was the father of the first house. He pushed me aside, went inside, and slammed the door shut. He held my shoulders tight and said never to talk again to Mia, or to any of them. I was shaking, so was he. There was no anger in his face. Only something like fear. Before he left, he told me again to never talk to them, especially Mia, if I want to live.

Just writing about that is making my hand shake. getting harder to write. Good night.

April 5, 2015, Sn

Mama called Aling Pamela's telephone. Aling Pamela called me to her house to talk to Mama. I crossed the adjacent new home. The twins were playing marbles. They stopped when they saw me. The bald man also saw me and gave me a look. I nodded, but he replied with a sneer.

Mama told me they'd be home by tuesday, or Wednesday. Auntie died the other day. I told her so far everything's fine. Still have plenty of supplies.

By 8 in the night, someone knocked. It was Mia. She apologized and attempted to go inside. I pushed her, gently, away. I told her not to talk to me again. I slammed the door to her face. Quite satisfying to be honest. Like, BLAM! In your face!

April 6, 2015, M

I had a dream. I was lying in the floor. My limbs were cut off. I was surrounded with candles and burned-out matchsticks and people in black robes. They were chanting. I couldn't understand them.

One of them shouted. Then arms, all rotten, burst through the floor. The arms enveloped me. The nails dug into my skin. I was dragged down beneath the earth. Then I saw a big mouth. All teeth are razor-sharp. The arms let go of me. I fell into that mouth. Then I woke up.

While washing the dishes, someone knocked. It was Mia's relative to confronted me the other day. He filled me with infos. Ridiculous ones, about the new neighbors.

They are witches. Or cults. They look like normal people, but they serve a devil. Not The Devil, a devil. Their master is seldom hungry, but if their master is hungry, they must give him food. Their master only eats a certain kind of human. Mia was the charmer. If a man gave in to her seduction, that man is safe. But if a man refused, that man is food. The refusal is not just a result of a decision or discipline or purity. Inside that man is a power the devil eats.

I told him that is ridiculous. He ignored me and carried on.

He said he was just playing dumb. He pretends to be one of them. He is actually some sort of an investigator or something. But his mission was years ago. He's now a prisoner. Admitting his true intention is a death sentence for him and his family. His real family.

He asked me if I saw some matchsticks around my house. I said none. Relief washed over him. I asked him what's with the matchsticks. He told me it's a symbol of having an interest in someone. I didn't understand.

I guess he did not know about what happened between me and Mia, but he knew we are talking, that's why he confronted me.

I couldn't control my chuckle. He looked offended. He told me to be careful, to not talk to any of them, before he left.

What a nut.

April 7, 2015, T

I played basketball early. We lost.

I still can't stop thinking about yesterday. I don't know why did he tell me those things. He must be on medication or something. But I followed his advice not to talk to any of them.

I did not see the nutsack this day. Maybe he was caught warning me or something, so they had to kill him. Or you know, bring him to a mental hospital. If he's crazy, why is he free to roam the streets? Dangerous.

So for dinner, I burned the rice. Crap.

Since this is the last night I'm gonna be alone (if my family will return by tomorrow), me and my friends, including Jericho, drank. We talked about random craps. Whenever the topic made a u-turn to the new neighbors, I tried to change it. Most of the times, I succeeded. My friends did not notice my avoidance of the talks about our new neighbors. I went home kind of drunk. Ugh.

Time check: 2:00am. gosh. I should've written this in the next day's entry. Eh.. whatever.

Someone's knocking. Might be my parents and brother. That's pretty early.

Good night!

Chapter 4

The following pages are blank up to the end.

"That's it?" Jesse asked.

"Yes," his wife answered.

"Assuming that this is an authentic diary, why didn't you burn this? Why make a novel out of it?"

"I was the one who wrote it. Just in case I lost it, it's a message to whoever would find it."

"And how do you know it's a real thing? What if some random person only wrote random craps? Or what if it's unfinished because of a rational reason? Maybe he lost it. Maybe he ran out of ink, or maybe he changed the notebook because this one's damaged and the pages are wrinkled."

"Yes. There is no logical explanation to prove that that's a real diary. I can't prove it." She took the diary from her husband. "I had a dream the night I finished reading his story."

Chapter 5

She is alone in the bus. There is no driver, but the vehicle appears to be moving.

She is sitting in her favorite spot: at the back. In her lap is the notebook. Its cover is full of creases. She opens it and begins to read. As soon as she finishes, the pages flip on their own. She cries, not knowing why.

She feels a cold hand on her shoulder. It is a kid. It is Wilbert. She knows it. Wilbert's face is solemn. He himself is crying. "Tell the world about me," he says.

Linda doesn't move. She looks at the kid's face and she feels tremendous pity on him. She cries more, making the floods at the floor of the vehicle until it's up to her ankles. It is warm.

"I will," she says to Wilbert.

"Don't," Wilbert says. "Don't let the world know about me. No, tell me. No, don't."

"What?"

Then suddenly, there are two heads on Wilbert's body. He doesn't actually have a couple of heads; it is only fluctuating, or like a pendulum, swinging sideways in a small arc. His neck is like a spring.

"Tell my story don't please tell do not tell tell do not tell keep me secret tell the world about me do not tell the world about me."

Linda holds Wilbert's shoulder firmly. His head stops moving. His face is contorted like a crying child's, but there're no tears, only blood. She sees the blood drop on the flood of her own tears, making a loud dripping sound.

"I will do what you want," Linda says. "The world will and will not learn about you."

Then she hugs him. Wilbert hugs her back.

"I'm sorry. I'm sorry," she can feel Wilbert jerking as he cries. "I'm sorry." She caresses the back of his head, like he is her own son. "I'll always remember you."

"Keep it," Wilbert says quietly. "Keep my memory with you."

"I will. I will."

Chapter 6

That night, she woke up crying. The feel of Wilbert's hug lingered a bit, then it was forever gone.
That same night she began to write her third novel.

End

About the Author

Van Lawrence Umerez

Van Lawrence Umerez started writing novels and short stories when the pandemic hit The Philippines. So far, he has written two novels and created several comics books.

He's currently a college student taking Bachelor of Science in Information Technology course. He lives in Bulacan, Philippines with his family.

www.ingramcontent.com/pod-product-compliance
Lightning Source LLC
LaVergne TN
LVHW041219080526
838199LV00082B/1283